DEATH ON CLARE ISLAND

MARTHA GEANEY

TURLOUGH, NOLAN PUBLISHING

This is a work of fiction. All of the characters, organizations, and events portrayed in this novel are either products of the author's imagination or are used fictitiously.

DEATH ON CLARE ISLAND

Copyright © 2018 by Martha Geaney

Library of Congress Cataloging- in-Publication Data (TK)

Produced in the United States of America

10 9 8 7 6 5 4 3 2 1

First Edition

ISBN: 978-0-9600567-0-5

For requests and information, contact:—

Turlough, Nolan Publishing

The Villages, Florida 32162

Email: mgeaney@marthageaney.com

www.martha-geaney.com

ACKNOWLEDGMENTS

The idea for the book was born many years ago when I was healing after breast cancer. But for the encouragement from friends and colleagues, I might have left the story sitting on my laptop. There are so many to thank who have believed in me along the way.

In Ireland, there is my lifelong friend, Reverend Chas Guthrie, who read an early draft and told me to keep going.

My cousins, Evelyn, Anne, and Mary, who have always cheered me on throughout the ups and downs of career and family life.

In the United States, there is the Mahwah Writing Collective who read early chapters, providing encouragement and feedback.

Special thanks to Nick Johns, fellow writer and author, who read and made suggestions that strengthened the story.

Huge thanks to my friend, Jim Hipple, who not only allowed me to use his name but also read an early draft. Jim provided invaluable insights into how the police would handle a case like the one in this book.

Of course, to my editor, Wil Mara, who continues to amaze me with his enormous talent for seeing the positive in every challenge.

Finally, to Bill, who whenever I feel overwhelmed in this writing journey disagrees with me saying "I think you know what to do."

This book is dedicated to my father, Michael Geaney, who was always loving, always kind. His mother died in childbirth when he was two years old. She would have been proud of him.

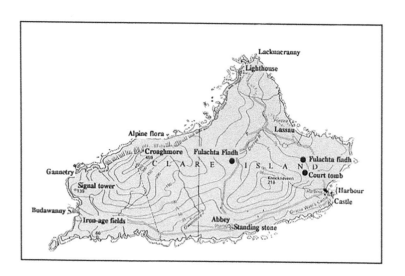

Lackuacranny

Lighthouse

Alpine flora

Lassau

Croaghmore   Fulachta Fiadh

C L A R E   I S L A N D   ● Fulachta fiadh

Gannetry   ● Court tomb

Signal tower   Harbour
°139   Castle

Budawanny   Iron-age fields   Abbey
                                              Standing stone

PROLOGUE

J ust a fifteen-minute boat ride from Roonagh on the west coast of Ireland, the towering mountain of Clare Island guards the entrance to the mouth of Clew Bay from the Atlantic Ocean. Gráinne Mhaol's castle sits on the rocky headland at the island's harbor. Most visitors come to view the scenery and the bottle-nose dolphins swimming in the bay. Others come to explore the archeological history, including the Cistercian Abbey where the 16th-century pirate queen is buried.

Matthew Sumner liked the five-hour walk around the island best of all: the danger of ignoring "Beware of Cliff Edges" signs that warned of falling to the rocky inlet below, the steep climb up Knockmore mountain, the view of Inisturk and Inisbofin islands from the peak, the small lakes, the potato lazybeds, and the Abbey Church. Oh, he would recommend any of the walks around Clare Island if pressed for an opinion. The shorter walks made more sense at the end of a day working in the Abbey ruins. Most of the time he selected the quickest route to the island's harbor and hotel, where he ate his evening meal, saving the full circuit of the island for weekends. But he wanted the solitude and shadows provided by Knockmore for tonight's excursion. He required the unobstructed view of the Atlantic Ocean.

As he made his way toward the southern side of the island, he took short strides, conserving his body movements to deflect attention. Zipping up his light jacket, he watched for small boats nearing the island, or for someone approaching him from the harbor. He was ready to slip on his stocking cap, making it difficult at a moment's notice for anyone to identify him.

Keeping this last point foremost, he felt for the cap in his pocket. Perhaps, he thought, he should put it on now, picturing his bleached blonde shaggy hair acting as a kind of beacon. It had been a cold, dull day, and it looked like a devil of an evening. The menacing dark sky to the east foretold the storm headed for the island. He could see the whitecaps rising angrily out of the sea as they bashed onto the beach. He scanned the bog and the coastline while his fingers continued touching the cap like a monk fingering his beads.

Intuition told him he'd soon find what he sought, so he resolved to brave the wind and impending storm. It was then he spotted a lone figure, head hunched below the shoulders. His first thoughts wavered between fear and hope that tonight's excursion would prove profitable. The person lifted a hand in salutation. Feeling a little puzzled by this, Matthew wondered why the individual he pursued would be friendly. He looked beyond the anonymous shape to the dark ocean. When he didn't see a boat, he immediately relaxed, thinking this was an islander out for an evening walk. In the few moments it took for the person to shorten the space between them, he heard his name whispered in the wind.

"Matthew, what are you doing out in this nasty weather?"

The voice, dull and sleepy, floated in the air between them like the hypnotic sounds of the sea. Loose, black clothing draped the person's frame, making it impossible for Matthew to discern whether it was a man or woman. His steps slowed. For in that moment, straining for a closer look, he understood too late that he had made a grave mistake. His final thoughts were of how much he wanted to live as the water choked off his breath. Then the darkness took him.

CHAPTER 1

Is there ever a good time to find the lost, the dead, or the missing? This is my mantra—maybe it's because of my own losses, maybe it's because this is just who I am, but I have always been for the lost souls.

THAT MORNING, THE SKY ROSE BEYOND THE SEA IN A LUMINOUS ultramarine palette, reminding me of Vermeer's *Woman in Blue Reading a Letter*. Treading the grassy path from the Clare Island Lighthouse bed and breakfast down to the harbor, I pictured my mother when she received a letter, many years ago, from Clare Island.

"Look Star, a letter from Ireland," she said when she extricated the mail from the tiny slot with her long, tapered fingers, her face lit up. "It's going to be a wonderful day."

That's why I was on Clare Island, which perches over Clew Bay off Ireland's western Atlantic coast. I was searching for my mother.

Squinting against the sun, I glimpsed a handful of people—adults and children alike—sprinkled along the beach. Picnic baskets, towels, and beach umbrellas dotted the sandy soil of the blue-flag seashore. The Clare Island ferry bobbed in the water as the day tourists and returning residents moved between the boat and the stone dock.

"Run!" someone yelled.

"Hurry up!" yelled another.

"Oh my God!"

"He looks dead!"

The words and cries reverberated up and down the mountain. Children abandoned shovels and pails, women gathered the kids up and scampered away, hands pointed frantically toward the beach. I jogged in that direction, nearly running past a man's body lying face down in the sand. Then someone in the crowd stepped forward and rolled him over onto his back. A large gash ran deep into his forehead. His blue eyes stared unblinking into the sky.

Have you ever wondered what the dead would say if they could speak? Would they pick up where they left off? Would they whisper or shout with joy that their voice could be heard again? And what if the dead in question had been murdered? Would they plead for their life, or try to change the words and deeds that led to the murderous moment? Would they admit their guilt and therefore be judged deserving of murder? Or would they pledge their innocence?

"Must have gotten too close to the edge of the cliffs," I said to no one in particular.

The man who rolled the body over rummaged through the pockets of the corpse's jeans, presumably looking for any kind of identification. The crowd gasped when he yanked out a cracked glass vial instead. Realizing I was in the wrong place at the wrong time, I spun around, intending to escape back to Clare Island Lighthouse, where I'd been staying. But a burly farmer, gripping a scythe in his right hand, stepped in front of me. He must have been using the scythe in one of the nearby fields and forgot to drop it when he ran toward the beach. Given the circumstances, the image of the grim reaper flashed through my mind.

"You should probably stay here, Miss," the grim reaper told me in what sounded like a Bavarian accent, "until the Gardai decide everyone can leave."

Guards, I thought to myself. *That's great.* Ever since the police decided that my mother's disappearance was a case of child abandonment, I've never trusted them. Still, I'm not one to argue with a guy holding a scythe. I stayed put. I had no idea then that by doing so, I became involved in a series of events which would result in someone else's death. In reality, I would come to know that greed, blind love, and infatuation caused the death.

But still I feel guilty.

CHAPTER 2

The corpse's pockets produced more data in the form of a driver's license—Matthew Sumner, aged 25, resident of Westport, County Mayo, Ireland. Some of the crowd recognized him, explaining that he rented a room at O'Grady's guest house.

"He's working on the Abbey Restoration." This voice came from a teenager, tears streaking her porcelain cheeks as she stared at his pasty face.

The Abbey Restoration project was being funded through government grants. Cistercian monks built the Abbey in the 1500s. The restoration project hoped to rebuild and restore it.

"I've often seen him with a dark-haired woman, walking along the beach," said the guy who'd rotated Matthew's body. "I may have seen them even yesterday." He emphasized the word yesterday as if he couldn't believe what lay before him.

At that moment, heart-wrenching sobs erupted from the teenager, her body shuddering.

"Come on, Lucia," said the older man standing next to her. He grabbed her hand and turned away from the crowd.

"No, I won't, no I won't," she repeated, shaking the hand

away with a ferocious strength that almost succeeded in knocking him over. "He taught me to paint!"

Her eyes scanned the crowd, but the elderly man grabbed her by the shoulders and pulled her away from the scene. As they withdrew, Lucia glanced back. Her eyes, tears streaming from them, were focused on the body.

"Aye, it's true. He works on the project," said the grim reaper.

"Where's Richard O'Malley?" someone else prompted. "He's heading up the dig. He'll know this chap well."

Heads swiveled and people rose on tiptoe searching for O'Malley, when a third person volunteered, "He's always here to meet the morning ferry."

More head twisting before the grim reaper said, "Well it doesn't look like he's here this morning."

The crowd provided scraps of information that clarified Matthew's role in the project. An artist by trade, his current project included researching the drawings on the Abbey's sacristy wall. Wind, rain, and sun had bleached the original etchings to ghostly afterimages. The Abbey's project committee employed Matthew to recreate the drawings and other art works belonging to the church.

The island's inhabitants and visitors remained in the harbor area until the police arrived. I mentally reviewed the option of leaving the scene or lingering in the area with everyone else. *Stay here!* is what the grim reaper had said. I decided that was the best option. Besides, my insatiable curiosity was getting the better of me.

FOR SEVERAL HOURS, THE LOCALS MILLED AROUND OUTSIDE THE shops and village cottages near the shoreline. Conversations buzzed with descriptions of hippies and drug users. I moved from group to group listening to what each had to say. Some of the locals cited the times Matthew wandered around the island's coves in the evenings. Others described him as quiet and detached. And no one paid attention to my presence. It was as if I were invisible.

I got restless and broke away for a walk along the beach. That's when I noticed Lucia's return to the drama. She lurked around the edge of the only road through the village, standing off to the side, never joining in the whispering or shaking of heads. Sometimes tears rolled down her face as she turned away from the little islands of gossip to plod along the beach. A few times, I glimpsed her staring up at the ragged edges of Knockmore's cliff.

"That poor girleen, she must be so lonely." Mrs. Leonard remarked. She was the owner of the Mace grocery shop near the quay, and my thirst prompted me to stop there for bottled water. In fact, it was the only store on the island with a liquor license.

She nodded toward Lucia.

"Who is she?" I asked.

"Lucia Cherisi. Have you ever heard tell of someone with a name like that? But that's her name. The family's not originally from here, you know. Unlike some of us."

"Oh? Where is she from?"

"Italy. An Italian fishing village. The three of them—mother, father, and daughter—arrived several years ago. No one knows why they chose Clare Island. They don't mix much and neither do we. The father's a salmon fisherman. I see him rowing out to his nets all the time." She glanced out the shop's window at the narrow road that rises from the quay up Knockmore mountain to the bed and breakfast. "Being a solitary operation, I can't imagine they make too much money. She's home schooled by the mother. And if you ask me, that's the ruin of the girl. No friends except for the dead painter. Most her age have girlfriends and boyfriends." Her voice rose as she placed the inflection on *boy*.

From the behavior I'd observed earlier on the beach, I figured Lucia wouldn't have much interest in boys. Set apart by her beauty and foreignness, I got the impression she chose solitude.

The shop keeper shook her head as she handed over my change. "Instead she mopes around the Abbey ruins. If you ask me, she knows more than she's telling." Then, seeing me glance first at the expensive looking two-row gold ring and, after that, the bandage on her left hand, she added. "It's nothing, just a scrape from a fall I took handling some of the delivery bags." She pointed to her left knee. "I scraped the knee in the process too."

"Have you lived here all your life then?"

"Since I married my husband, which is nigh on twenty years. He was born on the island. Aye. Two years since he passed but I have a lifetime of memories here that I don't want to leave."

I nodded. I didn't ask her if she'd known a woman named Maggie O'Malley. My mother would have been on the island almost ten years before this woman arrived.

THE GUARDS QUESTIONED PEOPLE ON THE BEACH NEAR WHERE THE body washed up, took names, and asked everyone to stay on the island for the next few days until after the coroner completed the inquest.

Damn, I said to myself, noting the absence of satellite reception. I'd expected wireless network coverage would be ubiquitous around the globe by now. No coverage meant no calls.

I tossed the useless mobile phone I'd purchased on this side of the Atlantic for making calls in Ireland into my knapsack.

Glancing over at my iPhone, I wished I'd arranged for international coverage. At least then I'd have been able to check my US emails and make calls. Totally disconnected! Can you imagine, even with two wireless devices—one of which was the most recent version of an iPhone—that I was actually cut off from anyone beyond this island?

So, during the two days following the discovery of Matthew's body, I passed the time rereading Troy Dunn's *Lost and Found: The Guide to Finding Family, Friends, and Loved Ones*. At least the weather was nice—golden sunshine and cloudless skies. When the news circulated that the inquest was over, everyone issued a sigh of collective relief, anticipating the normality of day trippers and vacationers ebbing and flowing from this remote island once again. Feeling jettisoned in more ways than one, I'd be happy to get back to the mainland and reconnected to satellite coverage.

Then a stranger approached me on the bed and breakfast's patio where I was seated, making notes from Dunn's book.

"Miss O'Brien?"

"Yes," I responded as my brain registered the fact that this person—a woman—knew my name.

"I'm Bridget Sumner, Matthew's sister."

"I'm so sorry—"

"Georgina Hill told me I could find you here," Bridget cut me off as she fumbled with some papers inside her oversized handbag. "I'd like you to investigate my brother's death."

I groaned inwardly.

"May I offer you a cup of tea?" I asked.

"No, I don't have time to stay. I'm on island to collect Matthew's body and take him back to Castlebar for burial." She drew a deep breath. "I should tell you that I believe neither the coroner's report nor the guards' assessment of what happened. Georgina said you help with these kinds of things. I hoped you'd agree to meet with me when you get back to Castlebar."

Although I had to admit that I shared her skepticism of the police's conclusion, I felt myself flush with impatience.

"What was the authority's analysis and final report?" I asked, even though I already knew the answer—*drugs*. That's what I heard on my visits to the shop for groceries. But I didn't have the heart to say that to the distraught woman standing in front of me.

Bridget smoothed the sleeves of her sweater as if trying to soothe herself. "They said he drowned and had trace amounts of cocaine in his system. It's their opinion that Matthew's death had the look of a drug user who fell from the cliffs."

"Did they tell you how they reached this conclusion? What did the coroner's report say?"

"An initial toxicology screen reported a trace amount of cocaine. That's crazy. Matthew didn't use drugs. I begged them to investigate further but they said it wasn't necessary." Her hands rubbed her sleeves again.

"I'm so sorry. It's never easy to accept the police's opinion, or anyone else's for that matter, about a family member." I touched her arm to show some kind of support. "Let me think about this," I continued. "I may be returning to the States in the next few days. I'll contact you when I get back to Castlebar."

Bridget's face hardened as she nodded in understanding.

"Fine. Well, thank you Miss O'Brien."

She held her head high as she turned on her heel and strode off.

I'm a researcher and information broker. My profession involves me looking into people's lives and sometimes disappearances and deaths. But we're talking long after the fact here. Fresh murders, however, are another story.

The Consulting Detective—that's the name of my company

—primarily researches lost birth certificates and marriage licenses. More than that, I sometimes find missing information about property and financial accounts so a will or an estate can be finalized. My work is accomplished by spending long hours scouring through public records, microfiche, obscure online databases, and so on.

My business began in my junior year at college when I tried to find my mother. After paying a company who made big promises but delivered little more than her name and the address we'd lived at before my sojourns in a series of foster homes, I started an information brokerage of my own.

Having access to data that most people don't has placed me at the heart of a mystery more times than I care to count. Private detectives and attorneys contact me on a regular basis. They usually want me to research documents and data related to divorce, adoption, family reunions, and missing heirs to estates and wills. Sometimes a family wants to make discreet inquiries—not wanting the particular relative to know that the family has initiated a search—about the status of a long-lost relative.

Isn't it ironic? Here I am digging into other people's lives, figuring out their personalities, getting into the heads of the missing, thinking about what drove them away from their families, and still I haven't located my own mother. My only solace in this quest is that I'm becoming better at what I do. I know I'll find her eventually.

But it's a mistake to label me a private investigator. While occasionally my research points the way to a murder, I am most definitely no Miss Marple. My name is Star O'Brien. I'm a 'Yank,' as the Irish say, temporarily living in Ireland for a couple of reasons. The first is the ongoing search for my mother. And the second is because my significant other, Dylan Hill, recently died of a massive heart attack. The attending cardiologist called it a 'widow maker.' I prefer to think of it as a dark, silent loss.

I was left with his half of our joint assets and all of his remaining estate in his will. You can imagine my surprise that his estate included French Hill cottage, Castlebar, County Mayo. We'd known each other for six years and lived together for half that time and he never once mentioned an Irish address. Was it a secret or an oversight? I don't know, but I mean to find out. Because some secrets, I have found, live parallel and undiscovered lives.

CHAPTER 3

I arrived in Ireland six months prior to my stay on Clare
Island. Most days I like it; other days I'm not so sure. I like
the wild gales that rattle the cottage windows and doors at
night. I love the rainbows that form each morning.

These opposing elements symbolize how I've felt for a long
time now. Sometimes I am fragile, as if my life could shatter
into a million pieces at any moment. Other times I forget the
sadness and yearn to move on with my life in the US. If not for
Dylan's Aunt Georgina, I would have returned to the States by
now. She is determined to keep me here since, according to her,
there's "not a soul" in the States whom I can call family.

Truthfully, I don't give a damn about claiming French Hill
cottage. What I want more than anything is to find my mother.
She vanished two days after my sixth birthday, without a word,
a note, or a goodbye. I remember the silence that greeted me
that morning when I awoke and raced out of my tiny bedroom
eager for her daily dose of hugs and kisses. But she didn't
deliver those embraces that day or since. Instead, I sat at the
kitchen table listening to the recurring clicks of the clock
growing louder in the dark silence engulfing me. The hours
beat away until the shadows cast by our few belongings merged

into the darkness. Finally, I rose, opened our apartment door, and rang Mrs. Mueller's bell.

Abandoned. That's what the police said!

But I didn't believe it then, and now I'm determined to prove it isn't true.

MY MOTHER DIDN'T SPEAK ABOUT MY FATHER, WHOM I NEVER met, although it's a safe bet he too came from the Emerald Isle. There are enough freckles on my face for two maps of Ireland. I spent time in a series of foster homes until the angels intervened and I ended up within a foster-to-adopt-home with the O'Brien's, who completed the official paperwork when I was ten.

Fate assaulted me again two months after my eighteenth birthday. I was supposed to be with them that day. Getting the call about the Cessna's crash was like going back in time. In one moment, I was abandoned again. But in life the O'Brien's had surrounded me with love, so in death their memory sustained me.

One thing I made a point of keeping from Bridget was that I'd already decided to make inquiries about Matthew. I didn't like the way the guards took it for granted that he was a drug user. Guilty or not, they and everyone on Clare Island branded him as if anything else good he'd done in his life washed away in the water. *As if he'd been abandoned*, I couldn't help feeling.

I knew they were wrong about my mother, and the same gut instinct told me they were probably wrong about Matthew. So, I'd learn what I could about him and what he had to say in life and in death, and perhaps come to a different conclusion than they did.

CHAPTER 4

I didn't sleep much the nights after Matthew's body was found. Tossing and turning, I couldn't stop thinking about wakes and funerals and other mortal endings.

The night after Bridget's visit was much the same. It just brought different thoughts about the police's speedy conclusions concerning Matthew's death. Finally, unable to take it any longer, I threw back the covers and leapt out of bed. Poised almost five hundred feet above the cold Atlantic Ocean in one of the two original lighthouse keeper's cottages, I lingered over my morning tea, watching the gannets swirling and diving for their breakfast.

I remembered my mother saying she'd lived on Clare Island for a summer with the O'Malley family so I booked one of the lighthouse cottages for a weekend, hoping to find someone who remembered her. However, just about everyone on the island is an O'Malley. Even with spending more time on the island because of the investigation regarding Matthew's death, I hadn't gathered any more information than when I arrived.

I finished breakfast and packed without hearing any stirrings from my neighbor, who lived in the adjacent cottage. Trying not to wake him with the sound of my feet crunching on the gravel covered courtyard, I then tiptoed through the garden and straight to the compound's gate. I was anxious to get back to Castlebar to check voice mail, email, and see Aunt Georgina.

The day promised a sky unfettered by clouds. As I picked my way down the steep and grassy track from the lighthouse toward the harbor, I saw the ferry *Ocean Star* working its way to shore. To my left, Achill Island and Clew Bay shimmered in the sun. The sheep with whom I shared the path ignored me as always. Ever-present, they dotted the landscape while also reminding me of the lunch conversation I'd shared the day before with the manicured Peter Hughes—

"Excuse me, I hate to intrude but I heard your American accent," he said, introducing himself.

I'd answered the knock on the door with the expectation of another visitor sent by Aunt Georgina. Instead, the man whom I'd seen coming and going from the adjacent cottage stood on my doorstep.

"You know on the beach the other day," he said. "That horrible business with the artist. Well, I was in the crowd and heard you speak. That's when I realized we were kindred Americans!" He stopped and extended his hand. "I'm Peter Hughes, owner of the cottage next door."

Overcoming my initial surprise, I introduced myself, and for a few minutes we talked about the glorious weather on an island where the tourist brochures made a point to warn visitors always to bring rain gear.

"Would you have lunch with me?" he then asked cheerfully. "I've made a few sandwiches, and we can have them out on my patio if you like. It's not often anyone stays in this cottage. And never a fellow American."

For someone living on a remote island where the residents fished and raised sheep, his polished finger nails, tailored slacks, and jacket certainly set him apart. So, out of curiosity, I accepted his invitation. Besides, it would keep me from fidgeting and reaching for my lime- green cellphone case and the mobile phone every few seconds to check for satellite reception.

Over homemade brown bread slathered with butter, plus lettuce, tomato, cheese, and ham, he described his business. Ex-Navy and former real-estate agent dealing in antique furniture that people in the United States and Europe commissioned him to find.

"Why Ireland?" I asked. I couldn't stop myself. I was sizing him up. I imagined him living in a place like San Diego in a multimillion-dollar house instead of atop a mountain on a dot of an island in the Atlantic Ocean.

"Grandparents. My grandfather was Irish. When I visited here a few years ago to explore my roots, I discovered a booming economy, and through him I found I could claim Irish citizenship. A European Union passport makes traveling easy." His ebony eyes pivoted toward the vast Atlantic as he told his story.

"Don't you feel isolated?" I asked, dusting sandwich crumbs off my hands. "How do you stay in touch with your clients and friends in the States?"

"Don't judge the book by its cover." He laughed, twisting the silver link bracelet on his right wrist. "My cottage has all the equipment I need to publish my monthly antique furniture newsletter, *The Lighthouse Link*, electronically. "Besides," he grinned as he refilled my water glass and pointed to the sheep dotting the landscape, "is there anywhere on Earth more beautiful than this?"

"The scenery *is* captivating." I said.

We agreed to keep in touch, although I didn't believe I'd initiate the contact. I hadn't made my mind up about Peter. The Ralph Lauren wardrobe, for example, struck me as somewhat vain. But then being ex-Navy, he'd have been trained to be careful about how he dresses and carries himself, even as a civilian.

THE *OCEAN STAR*'S CAPTAIN WAVED ME ON BOARD AS SOON AS I arrived at the harbor. As the only passenger, I choose a seat near the front, close to the cockpit. The ferry carries its passengers from the island to Roonagh Quay on the mainland. From there it'll be about a forty five-minute car ride east to Castlebar.

As we glided across the water, the morning air caressed my face. Closing my eyes, I imagined for the millionth time what my mother would look like now. What changes had fate and time made to her face? Would it match my memory of her as well as the worn and crinkled snapshot taken in the arcade at Coney Island? Uncertain, I extracted the photo from my wallet. I fingered its border and gazed at her smiling face, framed with short, wavy, thick, black hair. Her dark eyes had crinkle lines around the edges, as if she'd spent her life laughing and didn't have a care in the world. I wondered, of course, if she was still alive, and if she would remember the story she'd once told me about why she named me Star—

"*You know where your name came from, don't you?*" *She'd ask me, tousling my hair. I knew the answer by heart.* "Yes," *I'd nod in agreement.* "I'm named after a star."

"*That's right little one. A very special star, from Achill.*"

In my searching, I learned about the Star of Achill, a white crystal found on Achill Island. Local legend says that when people left their home, they climbed to the top of Slievemore Mountain on the eve of their departure and cried. When they descended, they selected a piece of crystal to take for luck. I imagined my mother chose my name because she believed I would bring *her* luck.

"You look familiar," the captain's voice broke into my thoughts. "Do you live on the island?"

"No, I'm a visitor."

"Aye, you may only be a visitor lass, but you look quite like a native," he said, scratching his head as if he didn't believe me.

"Why is that? Do I remind you of someone whom you knew on the island?"

"No. Not anyone I can recall knowing at the moment. It's just that you look Irish. That's all. My name's Charles O'Malley, by the way."

"Star O'Brien. Nice to meet you, Captain."

Not another O'Malley, I thought. Isn't it strange? Like some kind of twisted humor, fate had given my mother a common surname. Why couldn't it have been something unique like Gunshanon or Creagh?

"How about joining me here in the cockpit?" he asked. "Since you're my only passenger, I'll give you a tour of the ship's navigation instruments." As I rose from my seat, he picked up some magazines with the title *Subsea* and moved them into a storage locker. Patting the seat where the magazines had been, he said, "I've made some room for you."

While the ferry moved across the water, he explained how easy it is to determine the location of rocks and shoals. Circular shapes, numbers, and compass indicators moved across the surface of the cockpit's dashboard depicting the topography that the boat traversed on its way to the mainland. He caressed the instruments in a familiar manner. Smiling and whistling, checking charts and scanning the horizon, he portrayed a man happily intrigued with his gadgets and even happier to show them off. After a few minutes, he got busy with the business of piloting the ferry safely in to the dock and I went back to my thoughts.

Had Matthew owned a boat? I wondered. Anyone who contemplated moving drugs on and off the island needed one, as well as a working knowledge of the surrounding waters. Of course, there might be other ways to transport them, such as the ferry itself. That runs twice a day in the summer. The island's helipad was used to transport the residents during medical and weather emergencies. But I suspected that if Matthew really had been involved in a drug operation, it wasn't through an easily watched location like a landing strip. And why else would he have been seen going in and out of the coves so often?

As the captain brought the ferry closer to Roonagh Quay, I could see the ticket stubs, candy wrappers, and aluminum cans that littered the stone pier. The young boy who manned the ticket office bustled about the dock preparing it for our arrival. After the captain guided the ferry into its berth, they hitched the boat to its moorings within minutes.

In no time, I spotted my second-hand green Renault 21 touring sedan in the otherwise sparsely occupied parking lot. Since I hadn't known how long I'd be in Ireland, I decided that ownership was a better bargain than renting. The car had numerous dents, a manual transmission, and no power steering. On the other hand, its turbocharged engine efficiently powered through the dips and twists of the narrow Irish roads.

It hadn't taken me long to realize assertiveness as an Irish driving trait. When two drivers faced each other on a narrow byroad, it became a test of wills to see who would pull over first. I'd already driven my car into a ditch several times, which accounted for some of the aforementioned dents.

I glimpsed clouds covering the rugged peak of Croagh Patrick as I drove the thirty-plus miles from Roonagh Quay to Castlebar through the series of towns and villages: Louisburg, Murrisk, Lecanvey, that dot the western coast of Ireland, with Clew Bay on one side and the Connemara Mountains on the other.

Also known as the Reek, Croagh Patrick is named in honor

of Saint Patrick. According to tradition, he spent forty days and nights atop the mountain, praying and fasting. It's also famous for a seam of gold found in the 1980s. I remembered reading a recent news story about a man and a woman who were arrested for illegally prospecting. They were caught with picks, shovels, sifting pans, and a metal detector as they drove out of the mountain's carpark toward one of Murrisk's beaches. A pencil tip-sized nugget was hidden in a plastic bag tucked into a corner of their trunk. The police made the discovery when they stopped the car for a broken taillight. As I continued on the road through Westport to Castlebar, I couldn't help shaking my head.

LIKE MANY OTHER IRISH COMMUNITIES, CASTLEBAR IS A CITY whose beginnings date from the 1600s. Most of the buildings along Main Street originated around that time. But modern Castlebar also contrasts with the days of yore. Pharmaceutical and technology firms, for example, as well as railway access to Dublin have contributed to the town's growth and continuously sprawling housing developments. And if you're wondering how I know all this, it's because of the researcher in me. I can't help myself. I'm an information junkie.

The first thing I did when I arrived back in town was drive by Aunt Georgina's dress shop, 'The Golden Thread,' on Main Street. I zigzagged through the maze of streets to park in the alley behind her shop. Rather than walk around to the front entrance, I entered through the back door.

Georgina smiled the moment she saw me. "Star, darling, you look exhausted! Can I get you a cup of hot tea?" She and her assistant were working on a new dress display for the shop window.

"I'm not looking for hospitality," I said. "I'm looking for

answers. Why did you tell Bridget Sumner that I'd investigate her brother's death?" I frowned as I plunked down into the bulky but comfortable white leather chair near the front window. It was a perfect place for a husband or boyfriend while a wife or girlfriend shopped.

"I didn't do any such thing," she said as she handed the dress materials to her assistant and placed a mug of water into the microwave. "I merely told her that you were experienced in these types of things and that you enjoy helping people in distress. That's what you do, isn't it?" I do have to say, Aunt Georgina was one of the few people, other than lawyers and private investigators, who had some understanding of what I did for a living.

"You're somewhat right about that," I nodded. "The Consulting Detective's activities often lead to finding individuals who were presumed missing, and why they disappeared to begin with."

Ignoring my previous refusal of a cup of tea, Georgina handed me a steaming cup of Solaris Peppermint Delight, then placed herself on the shop's window seat.

"So, what's the problem," she said. "This is a similar situation, isn't it?"

I stirred the tea and took a sip. "Not quite. Normally in the States, a private investigator doesn't hire me to solve a murder. I don't usually interview people or conduct surveillance. I resell information that I research from databases, and often without so much as a name to go on for finding missing heirs and adoption searches." I shifted my weight in the chair, which was turning out to be less comfortable than I originally estimated.

"I want to know Matthew's side of the story," I then went on. "Not so I can solve his murder, if that's what it happens to be, but to give him a voice. Besides I'm annoyed with the police's lack of interest in learning what took place. I mean, even though they considered him an insignificant drug user, doesn't he still deserve justice?"

"Drug user!" Aunt Georgina shook her head. "There's no way that ladeen was involved in that kind of trouble!"

I took another sip of the tea. "Anyway, it's all moot because I'm packing up and leaving Ireland in the next few days."

Georgina basically jumped from her seat, "Leaving?! When someone needs your help? Star, I don't think you can do that!"

"I just want to find my mother," I told her, "or at the very least find out what happened to her. I've lost everyone I've loved. Some days I don't think I have it in me to suffer through any more losses!"

Resting her hand on my shoulder, Aunt Georgina held my gaze with her eyes. "Stop feeling sorry for yourself," she said. "You're an attractive and wealthy young woman. Others aren't nearly as fortunate. Your success brings with it a responsibility to the world community. And right now, the community you're in is Castlebar. So, let me tell you what I know about this terrible situation."

I regarded this sixty-two-year-old woman who knew everyone in the countryside. Today she wore a chic long-sleeve belted olive-green shirtdress with a matching scarf tossed casually around her neck. The colors highlighted her olive skin and brown eyes. And I realized she was right. The O'Brien's ingrained into my head the Irish trait of leaving the world a better place as a result of being in it. *'You have more than others, Star, and as a result you carry more responsibility'* my adoptive parents had said more than once. It was undeniable how their words echoed Aunt Georgina's.

But what about other people's responsibility to me? I couldn't help wondering.

I shrugged in resignation and said, "I'll have another peppermint tea, if you don't mind."

Aunt Georgina hastened to the back of the shop to fulfill my request. As she did so, she explained that Matthew Sumner was engaged to a highly successful financial advisor named Sharon Dawson.

"I don't think he would have jeopardized their relationship," she said as she handed one of the tea cups to me. "I wonder if she was at the inquest? Anyway, first things first. I've made a dinner appointment for you with Bridget tonight at the Davitt. She'll be there at 7:00 p.m." Then she grinned at me over the top of her cup. "Speaking of the time, I'm late for an appointment of my own. So, I'll see you later."

She set down her cup and hurried out the door, leaving me and her assistant shaking our heads at each other.

CHAPTER 5

This wasn't the first time Aunt Georgina made an appointment for me. I'd spent most of my life building a tough external shell to cover my vulnerability. And that meant protecting my independence fiercely. But with Aunt Georgina it's been different. With so many losses in my life, I have to admit I enjoyed the idea that someone cared about me again.

After using the local internet café to check my email, I stood on Main Street gazing longingly at an appetizing box of Cadbury's Roses chocolates in one of the shop windows. Then someone said, "Do you think it's a good idea, Miss O'Brien, to stare at a box of chocolates?"

I knew that voice.

I turned and found myself looking into the blue eyes— behind his John Lennon-style glasses—that drew me to him. Lorcan McHale's tall frame looked slim in the khaki pants and navy button-down collar shirt that he wore under a time-worn leather jacket. I worked within myself to regain control, but it wasn't easy. Why did he always seem to materialize at my most embarrassing moments? Like now, when my hair was blown every which way from the sea voyage and my wrinkled tee shirt had escaped from the confines of my Capri pants. Even worse, my nose caught the scent of sweat...*my* sweat.

"When are you planning to head back to the U.S?" he asked as he glanced down at a paper he was holding. His thick blonde hair scraped the top of his shirt collar as if challenging me to touch it.

"Leave Ireland? I have no intention of leaving, Mr. McHale. In fact, I have a new case and I'm determined to see it through."

There was a long silence as his face grew solemn and his eyes moved from his paper to studying me from over the rim of his glasses.

Why did I say that? I wondered. I already knew the answer, however. I planned on returning to the US as soon as I could, and if I did stay I wasn't going to try solving Matthew Sumner's death for Bridget. But Lorcan had that effect on me. I'm attracted to him, even though we have the kind of relationship where if he said black I'd say white.

"Look Star, I'm worried about your involvement in these cases of yours. How about having dinner with me tonight? You can tell me about it. I know some private investigators who might want to get involved." He folded the paper—which looked to me like a diagram—and placed it into his jacket pocket.

"Being the son of English aristocracy doesn't mean that you can tell me what to do," I told him. "I can take care of myself. And as for dinner, I already have an engagement."

I spun on my sand-filled and mud-splattered sneakers, held my head high, and fled away toward the car lot.

THE THREE-MILE DRIVE TO FRENCH HILL CALMED MY NERVES. Yes, I was attracted to Lorcan. But didn't *want* to like him. I questioned his motives.

Aunt Georgina told me Lorcan and Dylan had been friends once. Lorcan never mentioned Dylan. And Dylan spoke little of Lorcan. When he did, it was with a curious roll of the eyes and a "that guy's trouble." But as I'd discovered when Dylan died, he hadn't told me about many things, like French Hill cottage, which once served as the McHale estate's lodge. Never mind Lorcan! Why hadn't Dylan told me about French Hill?

French Hill sits on Lorcan's hundred-acre estate. His mother, Lady Marcella McHale, lives in the family residence with him. With my usual need to figure people out, I'd pictured her passing her days in their 18th century stone house, reading and having tea with her friends.

Boy had I been wrong! I met her for the first time at a dinner she hosted to benefit a local female politician. Aunt Georgina and Lady Marcella were on friendly terms, so when Georgina received the invitation to the dinner, she asked me to go with her. "It will be a way for you to meet some of the locals," she'd explained. When I was then introduced to the tall, thin, and blonde Lady Marcella, she'd hugged me as if we'd known each other all our lives. "Star," she said, "Georgina has been singing your praises since she learned you were coming to Ireland. We're so happy you're here! The West of Ireland needs independent women like you." Just when I think I know what someone is like and how they might behave, I learn something that causes me to reassess my initial observation.

As I neared the cottage, I drove faster along Cottage Road, a one-lane byroad which runs from the main road to French Hill. Walking from my car onto the cottage grounds, I always feel as if I am entering a secret garden. Maybe it's the hazelwood and ash trees that form a natural doorway through which I have to pass. Sometimes coming back to the cottage seems as if I'm being transported to an ancient Celtic kingdom. This was one of those times. The air felt cooler now, laced with a burst of rose-scented perfume from the bushes that lay recumbent against the stone wall. Pink, red, and white Sweet Williams and geraniums fluttered in the breeze, welcoming me home.

As I opened the door, I felt sad that I'd eventually be leaving this place. Two bedrooms, a kitchen, bathroom, and living room made for a cozy environment. Maybe it was the feeling of continuity I got from knowing that the antique mahogany, oak, and pine pieces in the bedrooms and living room had belonged to earlier generations of Dylan's family. I sensed a connection to him that made me feel quite at home when alone here at night, safe, secluded, and far from the worries of the world.

But it would only be a short time before fate shattered my security.

CHAPTER 6

There wasn't a parking space to be found on Kingsbridge Street as I drove past the restaurant. Further up the narrow incline of what I considered more of a lane than a street, I could see lines of people along the sidewalk outside Cody's funeral parlor. That explained the parking problems. Finally, I found a spot several blocks away and worried I'd be late, I grabbed my keys from the ignition and rushed to the Davitt.

The restaurant is named for the Irish rebel Michael Davitt. From what I've read, we were like-minded on many things. Mostly the fact that he fought for his ideals. Blood poisoning is what finally got him in 1906.

I chose the dining-room entrance rather than the pub door and looked around for Bridget. She was seated in one of the booths, folding up a bundle of papers that she then placed into her handbag. She glanced up, spotted me, and waved.

As I sat down across from her, I noted that she was dressed in a white silk blouse, tailored navy jacket, and black pants. It struck me that she wore her clothes like a uniform. She'd been clad similarly when we spoke on Clare Island, giving me the impression that her idea of dressing for success meant practical and ready-to-go. Aunt Georgina had filled me in on other details about her, including the Sumner family business—a button-mushroom farm outside of Castlebar. Bridget, who was thirty and single, managed the operation.

After exchanging pleasantries, we requested salad plates and a basket of brown bread. I also added a bowl of the home-made vegetable soup to my order. As soon as the waitress delivered our meals, Bridget directed the conversation to the matters at hand.

"My brother wasn't a drug user," she said right off as she tapped the table with her finger. "I don't care what the toxi-cology report says. How can the Gardai believe that he used drugs? They didn't even bother to find out more about him." She pursed her lips and looked down at the table before she continued. "He was a vegetarian, an animal-rights activist, a volunteer, and a religious person. Drugs were foreign to his beliefs. That's not how he lived his life." She raised her left hand toward the ceiling as she finished her sentence.

"Well, what else would people think?" I countered. "The circumstantial evidence certainly supports the police verdict. He had drugs on his body when he was found. He also had a gash on his head, and people noticed him walking around the harbor late at night and before sunrise." Not giving her a chance to respond, I threw out another question. "What about his boat?"

My eyes held hers while I watched her reaction. She main-tained the connection.

"Boat," she hesitated, saying the word slowly. "Matthew didn't own a boat."

"Did he have access to one? People noticed him around those coves."

"Well, the family owns a boat, and he borrowed it a few times. I'd take it out to him on the island and return on the ferry." There was a brief silence before she continued, "He wanted to take Sharon, his fiancée, out on the water during the long summer evenings, especially on the weekends when they both had a break from work. It was innocent, nothing more. Besides, he hadn't used the boat in several weeks." She used her fork to push her salad around her plate.

"Is it equipped with mapping devices?" I went on. I wasn't ready to let the subject go.

She shrugged and cast her eyes away from me. "Yes, the boat has a reliable GPS system." Her voice, I noticed, now lacked its previous intensity.

"Where is the boat kept?"

"Near Roonagh Quay in Louisburg, where the Clare Island ferry docks," she snapped, shooting a look at her watch.

Ignoring her testiness, I repeated my original question, "What else should people think about what happened?" I also made a mental note to look at the boat when I returned.

Bridget sighed, "Okay, I hear what you're saying about the circumstantial evidence. But Matthew wanted to be an artist since he was four years old. When it occurred to my parents that his taste for art and beautiful things was impractical, I encouraged him to follow his dreams. I supported him at art school when my parents refused." She emphasized the word 'I' as she simultaneously raised her left hand toward the ceiling. It was a gesture she'd used before, which seemed to be her way of stressing a point. Having demolished my soup and bread, I nodded for her to continue.

"He spent four years in New York going to school, had a show at Columbia University's Art Center in 1990, and taught art at Dublin College for two years when he returned from the US." She ticked off his accomplishments on her fingers as she spoke. "He'd just begun to make a name for himself restoring historical period paintings when he met Sharon. He moved back to Castlebar to be closer to her and devote more time to art history restorations. He was too dedicated to make a stupid mistake that could cost him his career. He had no time for drugs."

Her voice had raised an octave and her face was flushed by this point.

"Okay, then what other explanation is there for the evidence?" I prompted.

"I don't know the answer to that, which is why I want to hire you. Talk with Raymond Nolan. He heads up 'Save the People' where Matthew volunteered when he wasn't on Clare Island or with Sharon." Once again, she lifted her hand toward the ceiling.

"What, exactly, does this group do?" I asked.

"A fundamentalist group whose mission is to stamp out drug use, especially by children and teenagers. Matthew volunteered there for several years and he actively participated in fundraising events." She sighed. "I didn't agree with this part of his life. I mean being surrounded by people with drug dependencies can't be good for you. But he wouldn't listen to me."

I settled back against the velvet-covered booth and wondered about her motives. Not regarding her brother's death, but his life. Had she believed that much in his talent? Enough to risk her relationship with the rest of her family? It was unusual for a sibling to actively finance another in the face of parental disapproval. What had she to gain by encouraging Matthew's art career? She'd stayed close to home; so close that she oversaw the family business. Did she really want to know what happened to her brother, or was she seeking exoneration?

She suggested I meet Sharon. "What he saw in her, I can't fathom. I pleaded with him to break it off with her several times. He refused."

I nodded but said nothing. Listening, I have found is the best way to understand someone.

"Okay, you're going to think I was a jealous and controlling sister, never happy with her brother's girlfriends. That was not my motive. He's five years younger than I am. I felt responsible for him. But something's just not right with Sharon. She didn't even come to his funeral service, and she's been saying that she's not surprised about the drugs. I don't understand it. He worshipped her and would've done anything for her. I called her and asked her to contact the Gardai, request them to take a closer look at what happened to Matthew. She refused. Says she doesn't have time to waste on useless discussions with a woman who didn't even know her brother. Says Matthew kept secrets." Bridget exhaled deeply as her shoulders slumped. "Sharon has something to do with this. I just know it. What am I going to do? First, Matthew wouldn't confide in me. And, now Sharon has shut me out. Oh, God, I must have appeared so much like my parents to him at that point." She went back to smoothing the sleeves of her blouse.

"When was the last time you spoke with Matthew?"

"Just a few days prior to...." She turned away rather than say it. "He wanted to know if I'd loan him some money. I went out there, but he wouldn't tell me anything. Just said he had to raise cash." She fixed her gaze squarely on me. "So, are you going to help me or not?"

I released a long deep breath, fidgeting with the keys I'd put on the table when I arrived.

When I didn't answer right away, she said, "I hope 'S-O-B' doesn't mean what I think it might?" It was the first time that evening her voice carried a hint of lightness.

"What?" I realized then that she'd taken notice of my personalized keychain. "No, it stands for 'Star O'Brien.' But I'll admit I like the play on words." I smiled. "Okay look, I can interview Matthew's friends and use my research company to follow up on information I uncover. But I don't know how much good that will do. You still need to be prepared for bad news."

Bridget pulled her long black hair back from her face. It

was then that I noticed her red-rimmed eyes. For the first time that evening, she looked like a fragile young woman rather than a successful businesswoman.

"Did you loan him the money, by the way?" I asked.

"No. And don't ask me why I didn't. Maybe I'd gotten tired of playing the part of a surrogate parent. But I wish I had. Maybe he'd still be alive. Look, Matthew was my brother, Miss O'Brien. I loved him. He wasn't the person that everyone is describing, and I think that should be made clear. Please find the truth."

Opening her purse, she produced a check and pushed it across the table.

"This is for you," she said.

Picking it up, I read my name and the amount of €10,000.00. Then I slid the check back across the table.

"I can't take this from you. Not right now at least. I'll see what I can find out and keep track of extraordinary expenses. In the meantime, please get me the key to Matthew's apartment and written permission to board your family's boat. I'll let you know if I learn anything of interest."

She nodded, pursing her lips as she picked up the check.

"I'm sorry for your loss." I said as I rose from the table.

As I departed from the restaurant, I took a look back and saw that she remained seated, staring down at the check.

CHAPTER 7

As I drove along, I speculated why Bridget didn't hire a private investigator. With the money she was willing to throw around, finding one would be easy. Of course, a private investigator might discover that some of Bridget's motives were selfish. How were the family property and inheritance allocated between the two siblings? On the other hand, she'd been generous—according to her—when he wanted to go away to school. And she had gone to the trouble of seeking me out when she heard what I did for a living. Putting myself in her shoes, I'd want to get down to the truth too. Frustrated with the police's handling of Matthew's death and probably feeling betrayed by him on top of that, I figured she needed to know the whole story.

Then I asked myself why I wanted to take on this investigation. I still planned to leave in a few days. Was it fair to Bridget to commit to something that I might not finish? And what about my own commitment to find my mother? I admitted to myself that I wanted to prove the police were wrong about Matthew. And as for my mother, I'd never give up hope. *Never.* So that was my answer!

I was committed.

NIGHT HAD FALLEN BY THE TIME I RETURNED TO FRENCH HILL.
The only place to park there is on a patch of grass next to the
barn that sits about two hundred feet away from the cottage.
But at night, it might as well be two hundred miles. There are
no streetlights and no nearby house. Just me, the trees and
shrubs, the ancient stone walls, and the relentless darkness.

As I exited the car, the murky gloom emitted rustling noises
from behind the barn. I paused, and there it was again. I froze
for a moment to eliminate the crunching sounds of my shoes
on the gravel. But I couldn't help myself—I had to look.

As I crept around the side of the barn, my breathing came
in quick and shallow hitches. I peered around the back corner,
but there was nothing. Then the clamor started again, and this
time I saw its source. A large black sheet of plastic was hanging
from the outer wall of the barn, flapping against the wooden
skiffs that lay on the stone-studded ground. Inhaling deeply, I
headed toward the cottage. By the time I bolted the kitchen
door behind me, I was gasping for breath and could feel my
heart thundering in my ears.

Once inside, I checked the answering machine. There was a
message from Peter asking if I'd join him for dinner and a
concert in Castlebar on Sunday. His invitation reminded me of
the concerts that Dylan and I attended back in New Jersey. We
used to sit on the lawn under the stars. The first time we went,
he packed a thermos of iced tea and a bag of apples. I knew
then that I'd love him forever.

I decided to call Peter and tell him I'd go to dinner but not
the concert. I still wasn't sure I liked him. But since he lived
here, I had to determine whether he knew anything about
Matthew's walks around the island. Besides, I could always say
that I didn't feel well if I wanted to cut the dinner short. His

phone rang four times before it went to voicemail. I left a brief message saying I'd see him on Sunday.

After checking the remaining voice messages, I made peppermint tea and lit a turf fire in the living room. Every summer, Irish people cut the turf out of the earth in long rectangular blocks. I've seen people in the bog, cutting down into the turf and pulling it out. As the sods of turf piled behind the fender burned in a red blaze, I let the heat soothe my still trembling nerves.

Sequestered in this inner sanctum at the center of the cottage was like being wrapped in a cocoon, protected from life's intrusions. Two oversized Queen Anne wingback chairs bordered each side of the fireplace. I parked myself in one and reached for the Mead composition book that I kept for journal entries, notes, and conversations with clients. As the turf burned down and filled the grate with ashes, I wrote.

The writing process clarifies my intuitive notions as well as bits of information like a magnifying glass over small print. That night my notes reflected what I'd learned about Matthew so far, and the names of everyone I'd spoken with thus far. What would Matthew tell me if I could chat with him now? Whom would he want me to interview? His fiancée and Raymond Nolan topped the list, I was sure. After a few minutes, I'd developed a set of questions—How accurate was Bridget's perception of Matthew as the artistic do-gooder? With the demands of running a family business, she couldn't have had much time to know what was going on in his life. Would he agree with his sister's synopsis of it?

I finished my tea and Matthew's voice went silent. Now I'd have to sift through his belongings, his paintings, his books, and the emotions of the people who knew him in order to form a picture from the debris he'd left behind.

Some people don't leave much—like my mother, for example. I had few clues to follow in my search for her. The memory of the letter from Clare Island, her story about Achill Island and the origin of my name, and a family bible. But the back pages where births, deaths, and marriages would have been listed were ripped out. Had she done this, or someone else? And whomever it was, *why*? One thing was clear in my mind and my soul—the memory of her love—and the certainty that she had not abandoned me.

CHAPTER 8

Trudging out of bed at the sound of the seven o'clock alarm, I slipped into baggy sweatpants and an ancient gray sweatshirt. I'd slept in brief snatches interrupted by long periods of wakefulness in anticipation of my meeting with Raymond Nolan. Glimpsing the picture of my dog, Skipper, that I kept on the dresser did nothing to revitalize my energy. Instead my stomach tightened with pangs of guilt. My Belgian Schipperke stayed with friends back in the New Jersey town of Ridgewood. I'd call them later to check on him.

Rounding the gable of the house for my morning walk, I collided with a strong wind. This lifted my mood and gave me a reason to grin. With my body bent forward and my hair blown back, I imagined Cathy haunting the moors and fields in search of Heathcliff.

I had the road to myself as I approached the ruin of an abandoned one-room stone cottage. Sitting high in a field surrounded by tall grass and thorn bushes, the house fascinated me. Gazing up at the open doorway, I wondered how long it had been there and what had happened to its occupants. I'd developed the habit of climbing over the fence and walking up to the house each morning. When I neared it, I peered through one of the broken windows and imagined the family that once called it home. The children's heads bent over books, the father in front of the fireplace, a border collie lying at his feet, and the mother stepping around a table as she set out the evening meal.

Is this what my mother had known? Is that why she'd cried when she didn't think I overheard her? Had she missed her family? As I turned away from the imaginary scene inside the house to look down over the fields, a blur of movement caught my attention. I thought I'd been alone. Looking more closely, I glimpsed a fox's red tail as the animal made a hasty retreat over the fence and into the bushes.

Feeling rested after my walk and a shower, I drove into Castlebar to see Aunt Georgina. Ignoring Main Street, I zipped the car around to the parish church's parking lot and hoofed it to The Golden Thread. Georgina was busy showing a customer the new fall line of business suits as I stepped inside. I headed for the back of the store and brewed a peppermint tea.

Aunt Georgina's head appeared from behind a rack moments later. "I'll have coffee, black," she said. "Let me take care of this woman's purchases and I'll be right with you."

While I busied myself making the coffee, I picked up the tinkle of the bell over Georgina's front door. Now that her customer had gone, she was able to join me.

"What brings you into town this early in the morning?" she asked. "Aren't you supposed to be making calls regarding your mother?"

"Have you forgotten? I had dinner with Bridget Sumner last night." I told her. "I've agreed to talk to some of Matthew's friends and fiancée for her." I sipped the piping hot tea.

"Star, I'm so happy to hear you say that. I knew you'd do the right thing." She sampled the coffee and nodded her approval. "And you're getting better at making this."

"It's not a matter of right or wrong, Aunt Georgina. I'm

annoyed that the police didn't take more time to investigate what happened. There was a teenager involved. Her name is Lucia, and she used to hang out with Matthew on the island. If he was a drug user, wouldn't the police have wanted to ask her some questions? But they didn't."

"So, what can I do to help?

"Well, I want to begin with some of the people Matthew worked with. Bridget mentioned an organization called Save the People. I understand that Raymond Nolan heads it up. Is that correct?"

"Raymond Owen Nolan. He founded Save the People about eight years ago."

"What do you know about it?"

"It's one of the most well-known non-profits in the west of Ireland. Raymond's done a wonderful job developing counseling and support services for anyone who has a dependency, whether it's drugs or alcohol."

"Drugs. That sounds like a good place to start."

"Star, be careful how you approach Raymond Nolan. He's totally dedicated to his crusade. He won't entertain any hint that Matthew's death or the drugs found on his body are connected with Save the People."

"I'll be tactful, Aunt Georgina. What can you tell me about Nolan himself?"

"His family has lived in the area for years. They come from a parish called Prison."

I rolled my eyes at the inscrutable names that the Irish have for their villages and towns. From my reading, I learned that Irish parishes—the lowest denomination of government—began when England created workhouses for the poor. Obsolete now from a public-administration perspective, the parish names remain and continue to be used.

"Nolan's the oldest of four," Georgina went on. "He won a scholarship to Trinity College as a medical student. While he

was in Dublin, his youngest sister came to live with him. This
was when she started university as a music student." She shook
her head. "Somehow she got involved in the drug scene and
died of an overdose. Raymond blamed himself. He thought he
should have recognized the danger signs, especially with his
medical training. He dropped out of school and started the
foundation here in Castlebar. It's an obsession for him."

She stirred sugar into her coffee, which made me suspect
her comment about the improvement in my brewing skills.

"I suppose he'd want to be helpful since getting to the
bottom of this," I said, "would clear the foundation of any hint
of wrongdoing. Can I use your phone to call him?"

"Sure." She glanced at her watch as she gestured toward the
phone with her right hand. "Lord, look at the time. I've got an
appointment at the other end of town. I'll talk to you later,
Star."

She disappeared through the shop door.

RAYMOND NOLAN'S ADMINISTRATIVE ASSISTANT INFORMED ME I
could see him at two o'clock that afternoon. With several hours
to kill, I went to the library to discover as much as I could about
him and his organization.

Archived newspapers and microfiche contained stories and
pictures of various fundraising events. Many of the pictures, I
couldn't help noticing, were of Matthew Sumner and Sharon
Dawson, and not of Nolan. He may have been shy of the
camera, but not of raising money. The accompanying news articles painted a picture of a hard-working and dedicated man
who raised millions for his cause.

I was about to return the newspapers to the librarian when
I caught a glimpse of Peter's picture on one of the social pages.
He was featured in a story about a Chinese Auction to raise

money for a new MRI machine at the local hospital. The caption under the picture stated that his donations and support had ensured that the imaging equipment would be in operation six months sooner than expected. As I was leaving the library, I found myself reconsidering my first impression of Peter.

I arrived for my appointment to see Nolan a few minutes early. His offices were located in a two-story house on Church Street, right across from the Castlebar parish church. A long U-shaped driveway, lined with clay pots of begonias, geraniums, and mountain pinks, bordered the manicured lawn. The Georgian-style house presided at the top of a hill overlooking the town's bustling streets.

I rang the doorbell and opened the door, as the sign over the entry directed me to do. This took me into a large, square shaped reception area with an oak staircase at the back. I then scanned the décor—white paint on the walls, black and white tile on the floor, no pictures or furniture. *Stark* is the first word that came to mind.

A young woman who looked about twenty-five appeared and introduced herself as Susan Bell, Nolan's administrative assistant. She wore her jet-black hair parted in the middle and styled in a blunt cut to her chin. A gray sweater, short-pleated black skirt, and navy sneakers completed her ensemble. She led the way from the reception area into a large room on the left. I assumed this would have been the living room when the house was used as a residence. Now it served as her workspace. A sturdy-looking oak table commanded the center of the room. Brochures about the foundation, mailing envelopes, stamps, and other papers lay folded in precise stacks.

Susan informed me that Nolan ran late for appointments and that our meeting had been postponed another twenty minutes. I sat down in a comfortable armchair facing an open fireplace and asked about her time with the foundation. As she stuffed brochures into envelopes, she bubbled over with enthusiasm about her job and the wonderful things Nolan did for the community. Since she giggled and blushed beet red every time she mentioned his name, I speculated that she and Nolan might be romantically involved. But I changed my mind about that when she brought me into his office a short time later. I perused the room, taking in its details as quickly as I could.

Nolan was hunched over stacks of documents. Unlike Susan's area, this room had paper everywhere—on chairs, tables, the floor, and his desk. Some of the stacks towered over him, looking as if they might topple at any minute. Hadn't he ever heard of electronic databases and scanning devices?

Aunt Georgina had described Nolan as mid-thirties, but he looked older. His blonde hair had wide strokes of gray running through it. He didn't look particularly tall for a male—about five feet eight, I'd guess—and his frame looked bony and frail. Fine lines rimmed his eyes and mouth. I wouldn't have been surprised if someone told me that it had been years since he'd seen any sunlight. He reminded me of a mole burrowing into the earth, creating a mindless maze of tunnels. What was he hiding from? Had his sister's death left him that scarred, or was it something else?

He looked up from the piles and stared at me for several moments before rising and walking over and giving me a firm handshake. He wore jeans and a voluminous black tee shirt with 'Save the People Foundation' printed across the front.

"Miss O'Brien, I understand from my assistant that you're interested in the foundation. How can I help you?"

"That's correct. I'm investigating Matthew Sumner's death on behalf of his sister Bridget. I'd like to hear your impressions of him."

"You want to talk about Matthew." Nolan's face didn't change as he echoed my words. "There's nothing to talk about.

He's dead. The guards are satisfied. And so am I." Nolan wheeled around on his heel and moved back toward his desk.

"Yes, you're right. Officially, that is. However, there's quite a bit of talk because Matthew worked here, that the foundation was somehow involved. By answering some questions, Mr. Nolan, you'll be helping yourself." I moved some papers off a chair and sat down.

He shrugged his shoulders and shifted his gaze back to me. "Okay, I'll tell you what I can. In return I ask that you leave the foundation and me out of this investigation of yours. It will come to no good." He settled in behind his desk and said, "What do you want to know?"

Isn't it strange the way in which take-charge individuals like Nolan can shift moods so quickly? Did his abruptness mean he'd cooperate, or was he hiding something?

"Let's begin with what Matthew did here and how long he worked here."

"Matthew volunteered," he emphasized the word volunteered as if to contradict my use of the word work, "here on and off for about the last three years, ever since he returned from Dublin and met Sharon. The teenagers that he counseled loved him. His group drawing classes were always fully signed up and well attended. He used his artistic and creative abilities to draw the young people out of themselves and their problems. He initiated projects like keeping journals with pictures, songs, poems, things that they'd written. It was cathartic for them. Then about a year ago, he became secretive and withdrawn. He devoted less and less time to us."

"And did he give you any reasons for the change in his commitment?"

"No. At first I thought it was because his career picked up. He was supposed to have an art exhibit in Dublin this year. He was also serious about Sharon and with the engagement and everything else; I didn't give much heed to him not being here as often. But then I saw him at a fundraising dinner in June, and his appearance shocked me."

"Did you ask him about it? After all, he volunteered here. You must have had some kind of relationship with him." I emphasized the word relationship.

Nolan stared through me as if I weren't in the room. He picked up a pen from the desk with one hand and tapped the other in a slow and gentle rhythm.

"Yes, when I saw how thin he'd gotten, I went to his townhouse one night and asked him if he felt okay. He was rather nasty, as if we'd never known each other. He shouted at me to mind my own business. After that I didn't bother to ask any more questions."

"What do you think now?"

"I think he was a user. The symptoms were right in front of me. And now they're in front of everyone. My God, he had drugs in his system." The tapping escalated at this point. "Matthew fell prey to a terrible evil. It happens. Take my advice, Miss O'Brien. Leave it alone. And leave Save the People out of it."

Throwing the pen on his desk, Nolan then rose and walked over to open his office door for me.

Our meeting was over.

As I walked toward my car, a drenching downpour suddenly began. Trying to dodge the raindrops, my feet splashing through the rapidly accumulating puddles, I felt as damp and cold as everything else. A beggar woman approached me, wrapped in layers of blankets that, at the moment, looked appealing.

"Milk for the baby," she said over and over as she displayed one rough-skinned hand, cradling the infant in the other arm. I reached into my jacket pocket and dropped the euro that I keep for these occasions into her palm.

"Bless you," I could hear her repeating as I climbed into the car and headed back to French Hill cottage.

Seeing the woman reminded me of a call I wanted to make. Reaching for the cottage's wall phone (corded no less) as soon as I came through the kitchen door, I entered the number for the Parish Center in Bunnacurry on Achill Island. When the answering machine came on I hesitated, then decided to leave a message after all—

"Hello, my name is Star O'Brien. I'm looking for information regarding a woman named Margaret O'Malley. She was probably born around 1952. I'd like to make an appointment to meet with whomever looks after your church records." Then I left my phone number and my thanks.

After replacing the phone in its cradle, I lit the fires in the living room and kitchen, then changed out of my damp clothes. The silence that echoed throughout the rooms was deafening. Snapping on the radio, I settled in front of the living-room fireplace to think about my meeting with Raymond Nolan. Although my fingers itched to have access to my databases back in Ridgewood, I knew that real information breakthroughs came in following up with sources like Raymond, Sharon, and Lucia in person. Likewise, in my search for my mother, I had to look into every church and ancestry museum, and talk to as many people as I could, if I had any hope of getting lucky.

My intuition told me that Raymond knew more than he'd let on, and I expected we'd talk again.

In my mother's case, I wasn't so sure if I'd find out anything at all.

CHAPTER 9

Joyce, Shaw, Pearse, Yeats, and Bono have done a good job of creating an image of the Irish as intuitive, gifted, spiritual, and emotive. Perhaps the moderate climate's alliance with nature encourages the instinctive earthiness. This morning, the eight o'clock Mayo West radio show reported the temperature as ten degrees Celsius. Doubling the ten and then adding thirty, I loosely translated to fifty degrees Fahrenheit. The crisp air tickled my skin as my feet glided along. Ground fog, hovering at the foot of Nephin Mountain, shifted as elusively as a ghostly sprite. Both ends of a rainbow waned over its peak. Glancing around for someone to share the moment with and finding no one, I found myself missing Dylan.

When I got back to the cottage, there was another message from Peter, asking me to call him about our dinner. I hoped he wasn't going to end up being one of those needy guys who make a pest of themselves. While I was debating whether or not to call him back, the phone rang. I answered it, expecting to hear his voice. It wasn't him.

"I'm sorry for your trouble," Father Mulligan would go on to say, "but we haven't kept records here since the fire in 1976. It was before my time, but as far as I know whatever survived was boxed up and sent to the General Register Office in Dublin."

"What about the National School, Father? Wouldn't you have records of students?"

"The trouble is that everything was stored in Bunnacurry's church office before the fire. School records as well as those for marriage, birth, and death were destroyed. If you're looking for documents your best bet would be the General Register Office."

Isn't it odd, I thought, that the year my mother disappeared, a fire destroyed those church records? I couldn't help wondering if fate conspired to erase any evidence of her spirit other than what remained in my soul.

Not long after the call with Father Mulligan, the phone rang again. This time it was Peter.

"I just wanted to reconfirm tonight," he said.

"Yes, I should be back from Clare Island in time."

"You're coming to the island today?" He sounded surprised.

"Yes. Bridget Sumner asked me to look into her brother's death," I told him. "She's not convinced that the police did all they could. I'm going to interview Richard O'Malley." Glancing at my watch, I realized I'd better end this call or I wouldn't be going anywhere.

"Look, I've got to go," I said. "Is there anything else?"

"Just that I'll pick you up at 8:15 p.m. and..."

"Thanks." I ended the call, cutting off whatever Peter said next.

I BREEZED ALONG THE COAST ROAD TO THE CLARE ISLAND FERRY as if the devil was at my heels, making it through the departure gate with just a few minutes to spare. In the distance, shroud-like clouds covered Knockmore's summit. Shivering, I buttoned my pink cardigan, remembering that Matthew wore high-top sneakers, a tee shirt, jacket, and jeans when his body washed ashore. Without rain gear and hiking boots, not even residents choose to walk along the edge of the island's cliff. Had he planned on climbing Knockmore? If not, then why the nightly explorations? Maybe Richard O'Malley—a renowned historian, chronicler of the Cistercian monks' influence on the art and history of Ireland, and native of Clare Island—would provide these answers.

As the ferry glided across the water, I made a reminder to check into the financial background of Save the People. I'd have to call my office later to give them the background for the search. I'd also call Susan Bell to request a copy of the public data for the organization's finances.

I thought again about how much I missed access to digital databases. What did people do when they were disconnected this long?

Once the ferry docked and we disembarked, I pulled a map out of my knapsack to reorient myself. I trekked past Knocknaveen (the smaller of the island's two mountains) toward the Abbey, church, and cemetery, where legend says Grace O'Malley, the pirate queen, is buried. When she was alive, wherever Grace O'Malley went, she built a church for her loyal followers. Over two hundred men roved the sea under her command. These men had wives and children who lived on the islands around Clew Bay. What secrets did Grace keep, I wondered? She plundered British ships and built churches for her followers. Wasn't there a contradiction in that? What if my mother and I were descended from this Irish warrior princess? I liked that idea.

I walked along the road from the bay to the Abbey in forty-five minutes, noting a small shop and pub with the name—of course—of O'Malley. It was printed on the sign that hung over the door. New homes shared the landscape with so many old structures, including the lighthouse, Grace O'Malley's tower lookout, stone cairns, and bogs, mixing 21st century progress with the island's ageless wonder.

The island church was small and simple, embracing its altar and kneelers. It was also empty. I lingered for a few minutes, remembering the many times my mother and I attended Our Lady of Angel's Church in the Bronx. She always lit three candles. "Keep your eyes on the altar, Star," she'd say. And she'd scold me whenever I fidgeted. I asked her once about the three candles. She'd smiled and said "it's a light for the one who's not here." I don't know who she might have meant, but I've held her sentiment in my mind for a long time, imagining and believing that the light was for my father. And that we were separated for good reasons. But she never explained. The O'Briens and I attended Mass regularly, but once they were gone I stopped. It's not that I don't believe in God—it's that I don't think he's in churches. I like to think he's in the people and the angels we meet along our journey.

I left my memories behind and ventured around the back of the church. There was a graveyard and the half-standing remains of what once must have been the monks' abbey. Over to its right, a sign indicated to tourists that they perused the former abbey's sacristy. I lowered my head and crept cautiously into the small, stone-encased room. There was a man kneeling in front of a wall, like a monk lying prone in a moment of supplication before an altar. When my eyes finally adjusted to the dim light, I realized that he wielded a fine brush, similar in size and shape to a child's toothbrush, in his right hand. Using tracing paper, he went over and over the faint, ethereal lines of the hunting and wildlife scenes depicted on the wall.

"Excuse me," I said quietly, "can you tell me where I might find Richard O'Malley?" I inched my way even further into the claustrophobic space where the abbey's former inhabitants donned robes and prepared to celebrate rituals.

The man who turned to me was stocky and of medium

build. I would also describe him as a smaller version of what I'd always imagined Friar Tuck might look like. A curly brown beard enveloped his face, which smiled up at me. The smile extended to his dark brown eyes.

"O'Malley here," he said jovially.

"You're Richard O'Malley?" I stared at the sandals he wore in the midst of the rubble.

"Well, I'm definitely not the Abbot," he replied, beginning to set his brush into a leather pouch that he excavated from the depths of his Carhartt overalls. "Who are you?"

"I'm Star O'Brien. Bridget Sumner hired me to investigate her brother's death. I'd like to ask you a few questions if you don't mind."

"Aye, no problem." O'Malley's laughing brown eyes lost some of their glow. I could tell right away that this was a painful topic for him. "Just give me a moment."

He brushed off his hands, jumped to his feet, and motioned me to lead the way back out into the sunlight. Then he led me toward the stone wall that surrounded the abbey's graveyard.

"It's a very sad thing what happened to Matthew," he began softly. "I felt like he was one of me own." I smiled, noticing O'Malley's use of the word me instead of my—one of those ways of speaking that the Irish have. "Enormous talent that lad had. At times it struck me that the original monks had crossed over into Matthew's hands and mind. His work was that good! I'm positive he would have received awards for his efforts here when it was completed." O'Malley's voice quivered as he gazed toward the water that washed against the rocky shore.

"Were you on the island the day he died?" I asked.

"Aye, I was indeed. But I didn't see him." O'Malley paused before continuing. "I had a mountainous folder of paperwork related to the project's grant money that had to be completed. So, I spent the day at home in my cottage filling out forms and cursing bureaucracy."

"Okay, so what do *you* think happened to him?"

"Well, he was the victim of foul play, of course. Or it could have been a terrible accident. But these rumors about drugs are gossip and nothing else. A bunch of ignorant people with nothing good to say about anyone, even themselves." He twisted abruptly and spat over the wall. "You're not Irish, are you, Star?"

"No, I was born in the United States." I couldn't help wondering what was behind this question.

"No harm in that. You see, you need to understand that the people here are always willing to believe the worst of a person if that person is in any way different from them. And Matthew looked different. Like all artists, he experimented on himself. He sometimes wore a ring in his ear, dyed his hair all the colors of the rainbow, and had jewelry dangling from his belly button. Just recently, he'd inked his body with tattoos of classic art."

I nodded, having glimpsed the edges of a tattoo through the wet strands of hair that clung to his neck.

"I'm telling you, though, he was a fine lad where it mattered most."

"Had his behavior changed before his death?"

"Well, aye...I'd say so. He'd become quieter and more impatient. Now, his work hadn't suffered. That was still as good as ever. But he didn't joke around like he used to, and he took to going for long walks in the evening around the harbor. He also kept records of the tides, as if he expected something to happen."

"Did you ask him about it?"

"Aye, I did. He told me he absorbed the spirits and history of the area, imagining what it was like to be a monk living on a remote island, alone and close to nature but well-fed and educated." O'Malley paused to shift his weight against the wall's sharp stones. "'Richard,' he'd say, 'the waters around this island are not as pure as they look. They wash away the secrets of many sinners.'"

"What kind of secrets?"

He shook his head. "I don't know, lass. And I didn't pry."

"What do you know about his time with Save the People?" I asked as I laid my heavy knapsack on the ground.

"Not much, other than he had a knack for working with teenagers. Some of them used to visit the island. And to tell you the truth, I had no desire to know anything more about Matthew or any of his visitors. I'm mindful of me own business. And so should you be."

Seeing the puzzled look on my face, he continued.

"Drugs kill people, that's the bottom line. Matthew might have crossed the path of some tourists involved with narcotics. People use the isolation and solitude of the island to experiment. Or he might have simply fallen from the cliffs. Having grown up on the island, I know the dangers better than anyone. I wouldn't venture around the coves or the cliff edges after dark. Anything is possible."

O'Malley's voice dwindled into silence and, shaking his body, he then said, "I'm going to have a bit of lunch. Would you care to join me?" He gestured to a knapsack perched on one of the carved stones that was covering a grave.

Glancing at my watch, I realized I didn't have much time before the last ferry of the day returned to the mainland.

"No thank you, but I'd like to ask you one more question if I might."

"Sure."

"Since you're a native, I supposed you might remember or know something about a young girl who visited the island during the summers about thirty-five years ago. Oh, maybe some time between 1965 and 1970. Her name was Maggie O'Malley, and she came from Achill Island. I'd guess that you and she might be about the same age...?" I asked this tentatively because I didn't know how he'd react.

"No, no, I don't recall anyone by that name. Although that was a long time ago. You might want to visit Grace O'Malley. You probably passed her pub and shop on your way here. A descendant of our first beloved pirate queen." He chuckled. "She's the longest living resident of the island and knows everyone. Tell her that you spoke with me and she'll entertain your questions. Probably share a jug of hot whiskey with you at the same time."

"Are the two of you related?"

O'Malley roared laughing. "You'll soon learn that we're all related on this island. In more ways than one."

I nodded. "Okay, thank you, Richard. Now I've got to go or I'll be staying here for the night. I'll be back though with more questions." I picked up my knapsack and put my notebook and pen into one of its pouches.

"Any time, lass. I'll be in Dublin for a few days later this week, but I'll do anything I can to help give Matthew back his dignity and his reputation. Just be careful."

He turned away then, meandering slowly toward his restoration project before I could see if his eyes had regained their light.

I SPRINTED TOWARD THE HARBOR, CURSING MYSELF FOR WEARING my customary Rocket Dog flats. But I arrived just as the other passengers were boarding for the return trip to Roonagh Quay. I wouldn't have time to look for Grace O'Malley today. But as the ferry chugged away from the island, I wondered about the connecting webs among all the O'Malley's, both past and present. The ancient Grace O'Malley and her dedicated followers were ruthless and fearless in their control of Clare

Island and Clew Bay. There's even the story that Grace once attacked her own son when he sided with her enemy.

How much of the ancient O'Malley thirst for control flowed through Richard's veins? His Friar Tuck demeanor could be a disguise. He appeared to want to help clear Matthew's name. But then he also had his own interests to mind related to the funding of the Restoration project.

How far was he willing to go to protect them?

CHAPTER 10

When I returned to Castlebar, I called Bridget to see about getting into Matthew's studio apartment. She said she had the key as well as the written permission to board the Sumner family boat. We arranged to meet at The Golden Thread.

When I got there, Aunt Georgina was just closing up.

"Star, I'm so glad to see you," she said. "I hoped you'd stop by. How about having dinner together tonight? I'm not in the mood to cook."

I didn't respond right away because I noticed she was resting her short body against the shop's door.

"Are you okay, Aunt Georgina?"

"Nothing that a good night's sleep won't fix," she said. "Now let's get out of here before someone I know comes along."

'Well, do you have to leave just this minute?" I asked, then put on my biggest smile. "I need a favor."

"Oh, okay. Well, we don't have to leave right away. What do you want, Star?"

"I can't have dinner with you—I have another engagement. So, will you help me choose a dress? You're so good at picking outfits for me that I—"

Aunt Georgina was already reopening the door and tugging me inside.

"A beautiful maroon silk dress arrived today," she said. "It's perfect for you. It's got a sexy slit up the sides to accentuate your long legs. That's if you wear heels instead of those funky flats you love so much."

She glanced at my feet, shaking her head.

"The color will complement your black hair and pale skin," she went on. "I've never seen anyone with raven hair coupled with skin as pale as yours. With the freckles and hazel eyes, you are a throwback to the Celts. Except, of course, you're much taller."

She continued chattering about my general form and figure while she dashed to the store room, emerging moments later with the dress draped over her arm.

"Who's the dinner date with?" she asked, looking at me suggestively as she handed over the dress and gestured to the fitting room.

"Peter Hughes. I met him on Clare Island. He's an American who's been living here for a few years."

I slipped the dress over my head and went to the shop's dressing mirror. Aunt Georgina was right about it—I felt slim and slinky as the silk fell smoothly along my body.

Then I noticed Georgina's smile had faded away.

"What's wrong? Don't you like the dress?"

"I love the dress," she said. "You look beautiful. As you do in anything you wear. I just imagined you had a dinner date with Lorcan, that's all."

"Lorcan McHale? I don't think so."

"Why not, Star? He's handsome. Especially when he smiles. I just love the way his blue eyes light up behind those pewter rimmed glasses. Do you know that he's a pilot? He designs and flies kites...."

"Aunt Georgina, stop gushing," I interrupted. "I don't want

to hear one more word about Lorcan and your opinions about his many attributes. As far as I'm concerned he's nothing but arrogant and self-assured."

I could see Aunt Georgina's disappointment, so I clearly needed to reassure her.

"Anyway, this is not a romantic dinner. We're two Americans in a foreign country spending time with one another. That's all. And by the way, I'm saying yes, I'll take the dress. Just like on the American TV show."

As she rang it up, I imagined what it would be like to date again. Here I was buying a sexy dress to wear tonight, yet I certainly wasn't ready for the commitments and vulnerabilities that came with a deep relationship. Maybe I'd never be.

Just as I began telling Georgina about meeting up with Bridget, the shop bell jingled and in she walked.

"Miss O'Brien?" she called out, "are you here?"

Her flat voice and whispered words contrasted with the forceful and confident woman I'd met at the Davitt a few days before. Aunt Georgina and I stepped forward to greet her. Then, after she and Georgina exchanged a few words about Bridget's parents, we left. As I followed Bridget toward Westport —a seaside town and gateway to many of the west coast's beaches and coves—I contemplated her metamorphosis. Her faded spirit didn't suit her.

What had happened?

∼

MATTHEW'S UNIT STOOD IN THE LINE OF EIGHT TOWNHOUSES that comprised Clew Bay Quay Estates. Each one boasted a blue door, red-trimmed windows, and an awning over the front entryway. A shade hung in the living room window, keeping uninvited eyes from peering inside. Two other windows, also shuttered, closed, and unseeing, completed the symmetry of the front façade. Lanky black wrought iron 18th century style lamp posts rose up at the perimeter of the row, and dogwood trees sheltered the sidewalk. The back of the house faced Clew Bay, and the front the Asgard Bar, one of Westport's popular restaurants. This was a high-rent district. So, how had Matthew afforded it?

Musty air assaulted us when Bridget opened the front door. The darkened hallway that lay before us disappeared toward the back of the house. Wanting to form my own impressions, I asked her not to accompany me into the inky interior. The first thing that struck me as I neared the end of the hallway was the view from the deck. It was an artist's dream, providing a front row seat to the cyclical processes of nature—sunrises and sunsets. I climbed the stairs to the second floor, wanting to see Matthew's studio before anything else. I paused at the door before crossing the threshold. It was like stepping into a painting. Unlike the shuttered front of the building, the windows up here were naked, gazing out onto the southern shore and aquamarine waters of Clew Bay. To the left, Croagh Patrick's triangular summit ascended into low hanging clouds. And in the distance, Clare Island appeared to shimmer. In the foreground, a boat basin and repair yard provided human interest.

Back inside, artwork covered every inch of the walls: pencil sketches, oils, and watercolors. Half-used tubes of paint, dirty brushes, and a crusty palette lay on a table. An easel had been reposed in the middle of the room with an unfinished drawing on its shelf. In contrast to the warm landscapes outside, the drawing, in question, depicted roiling, turbulent, and funnel-shaped clouds painted red and black, rising from a boiling cauldron of water. It looked like an inescapable tornado about to crash onto land. My head swam as the image seemed to whirl before me. Closing my eyes, I sensed the painter's anger. Opening them again, I moved a few feet back to take in more of the piece. In addition to the dark background, a highly contrasting line—white, almost luminous—ran up through the center of the painting. Were the guards right about the drug use? I wondered then. Was this an experiment or an expression of something within Matthew? Had some kind of mental or physical illness begun to affect his creative judgment? I shivered—aware of the dankness from the empty rooms now settling under my skin—and headed back downstairs.

There wasn't much to see on the first floor. Matthew had been a neat housekeeper, with a minimum of belongings and general clutter. A veil of dust covered the furniture. A half-eaten biscuit lay on a plate in the sink. Some bills took up space on the kitchen table. I picked them up and found all the usual routine expenses. At the bottom of this pile was a brochure for a place called 'Tranquility House.' I was about to put it back, thinking it was a vacation getaway advertisement. Then the words "Drug Rehabilitation Clinic, Dublin" drew my attention. Shoving the brochure into my jacket pocket, I went in search of Bridget. She had since disappeared, and I eventually found her hunkered down in her car.

"I couldn't stand to be in there." She blinked her eyes in an effort to keep the tears from running down her face.

I nodded. "This seems like a pricey district given the view and easy access to the shore. How did Matthew buy this place on a struggling artist's income?"

"I loaned him the down payment and he paid me back a little at a time," she said. "Sometimes it was a struggle to get the money because he had the regular mortgage payments as well. Remember—although the work on Clare Island was prestigious, it didn't pay much. He had trouble making ends meet, but he still couldn't get another job because he gave so much of his time to the foundation." She pressed her lips together as she looked away, using one hand to knead the purse that sat on the passenger seat. "But I know he was good for it; he would have paid me back in time."

I wondered again if Bridget were as faithful to her brother as she appeared. It was just as easy to think she was secretly relieved that someone who needed considerable financial assistance was finally gone from her life, family ties notwithstanding.

"I'm finished," I told her. "Why don't I lock up for you? And then I'll follow you back to Castlebar. I'll hold on to the keys for a while if you don't mind."

She shook her head in agreement. "Okay, that's fine. I've also let the manager at Roonagh Quay know that you'll be stopping by to get access to the boat. Here's the written permission. Oh, and here's Matthew's diary...." She handed me a small spiralbound calendar. "I found it on our boat. It looks like he made some notes about tides around the island."

"Thanks."

Back in my car, I plucked the brochure out of my jacket pocket and tossed it on the passenger seat, making a mental note to call Tranquility House as soon as I could. When we got closer to Castlebar, Bridget angled off the main road toward the opposite side of town. I continued to the right, around the outskirts of town and in the direction of French Hill.

AUNT GEORGINA HAD BEEN KIND ENOUGH TO DELIVER THE NEW dress, which I found on my bed. I was elated to see that she'd also lit the fire in the living room. Tired, I suddenly longed to pass the evening in front of the flames while reading a good book rather than go out to dinner. This sentiment was compounded by the sight of the silky material now draped across my bed. I worried about giving Peter the wrong impression. I wanted to stay in my comfort zone—looking for what was lost. Was there something wrong with me? Or did I miss Dylan too much? I realized I didn't have an answer.

Impatient for action, I decided to call Tranquility House now. I did, making an appointment to see the administrator on Tuesday. After that I took time to wash my hair. As I lounged in front of the fireplace, towel-drying my short bob, I admitted to myself that I did harbor some attraction to Peter. And part of it, I knew, had to do with his philanthropic efforts, which were impressive.

The cuckoo clock in the kitchen interrupted my ruminations. This turned out to be advantageous, as it brought me swiftly back to rationality. What was I thinking? I didn't have the time or the heart for attachments. And as soon as I fulfilled my commitment to Bridget, I'd be on the next plane back to the United States. Furthermore, based on the news from the Achill parish priest, the dream of finding my birth mother here seemed more distant than ever.

Fifteen minutes later, as I was raking my fingers through my hair for the last time, the front doorbell rang. Peter certainly was punctual, I had to give him that.

I opened the door. Once again, his appearance was impeccable, everything pressed and every hair in place. He wore charcoal gray slacks, a white turtleneck and a navy jacket. The contrast of the turtleneck and jacket complemented his ebony eyes and black hair. I invited him in while I went to get my coat.

When we stepped outside, I was surprised to see an S-Class black Mercedes sedan. I'd figured him for something a bit smaller and less unobtrusive. I was about to ask him about his choice in cars and where he kept it. Then his arm curved around my back and gently guided me into the front seat.

Deciding to just enjoy the moment, I said nothing.

PETER HAD CHOSEN THE KIRK RESTAURANT, NAMED FOR ITS original function as a church. Built in 1863 for a congregation of

Presbyterians, which became extinct within thirty years, the building lay dormant until sometime in the 1950s when the interior was refurbished and transformed into a family-owned restaurant through several generations.

We followed the waiter up a set of stone steps to the balcony, which looked as though it formerly served as the church's nave. Flickering tea lights cast shadows against the stone walls. Other couples occupying the few tables leaned in toward each other, speaking in hushed voices. Faint strains of violins, fiddles, and uilleann pipes colored the air.

My breathing deepened and slowed as I inhaled the intimacy of the setting. The musical echoes of history tugged at my heart, and my mind wandered to the future, imagining what it would be like to fall in love again.

"Star, you look beautiful," Peter said, looking up from the menu and fixing his gaze on me. "I'm happy you agreed to have dinner with me. I don't get off Clare Island enough."

"To be honest," I replied, "I almost canceled dinner. Looking into Matthew's life has kept me busy the last few days. I'm so tired I was tempted to call it an early night."

"Yes, I tried to ask you about that earlier when we were on the phone. But you rang off so quickly.... So, what's this all about? You said you're investigating Matthew Sumner's death?"

"Yes. Aunt Georgina told Matthew's sister, Bridget, about my work as a researcher and information broker," I looked down at my ever-present—although at present not-particularly-useful —lime-green case which held my phone. "She's asked me to see if I could learn anything more about Matthew than what the police uncovered. She doesn't accept their decision that this was a low-level drug incident gone wrong."

"That's absurd. Why would she question their judgement? And what does she expect you to do?"

"I don't know what I can do other than ask questions and interview people who knew Matthew." I paused to butter the crusty roll, the waiter had left on my bread plate. "What about you? Did you ever meet Matthew during one of his walks around Clare Island?"

"Me?" Peter laughed. "No way. I'm not one of them, as they like to say out there." He raised his eyebrows. "As far as the natives are concerned, this Yank is still a stranger, even after three years. Other than the odd hello at the shop when I'm picking up groceries, everyone ignores me."

I nodded and remembered how, after Matthew's body was found, I was able to drift in and out of the groups on the beach and no one acknowledged me.

Peter continued, "Well, I'm glad you changed your mind about not cancelling dinner. Do you have any ideas about how Sumner came into possession of the drugs they found on his body?"

"Nothing other than what the police surmised," I replied. "That he was a low-level user. But I found a brochure for a drug rehabilitation center in his townhouse. I'm driving to Dublin on Tuesday to see if there's any connection." I closed my menu, having decided on the wild Irish salmon.

"Why don't we go together then? I haven't had a break from the island in months. Besides, I have to confess that I'd use any excuse to spend more time with you." He reached across and gently squeezed my hand before taking up his glass of water.

"Well," I said, enjoying the warmth of his touch in spite of my reservations. "It's a long ride, and I'd enjoy having company. So, I'll make you a deal. I'll bring lunch if you do the driving." I surprised myself with this. Maybe it was the romantic setting, but I suddenly looked forward to spending more time with him.

"Done," he said with a smile.

∾

DINNER ARRIVED AND I FILLED HIM IN ON WHAT I'D LEARNED SO far about Matthew from his sister and Richard O'Malley. It wasn't much, I realized. Peter's hand beat a rhythm on the table while he listened, and I appreciated his attentiveness. Unlike Lorcan, Peter didn't try to discourage me from the investigation.

When I finished, he nodded slowly and said, "So you haven't made much headway yet."

"No. It's been slow going thus far. But I just don't believe that Matthew was a user. He's been too productive not to have been clean."

"I've heard that he was up and coming in art circles. Hasn't anyone considered that he just might have lost his footing while sketching or something? It happens quite often. That's one of the reasons for the island's helipad." He shook his head before continuing, "As a former navy man, I wouldn't go as close to those cliffs as I see so many others do."

The waiter came over then and took down our dessert order. Then I asked Peter about his business and whether he enjoyed it.

"Enjoy it," he laughed. "I love it, Star. Imagine a child whose father's motto was 'spare the rod, spoil the child.' My father was a doctor and we were wealthy. But he didn't believe in spending his money. When everyone else in high school received a Mustang convertible for graduation, my father bought me a bicycle."

Dessert came, and he was soon savoring every bite of his carrot cake.

"So here I am now, enjoying a wealth that I never imagined. And even more importantly, the freedom to come and go as I please doing something that I love. There's a lot of truth in that old saying 'wherever you go, go with all your heart'."

I smiled—that explained the Mercedes.

"But why antiques? And why a newsletter?"

"Well, after college and my navy service, I went into real

estate and realized that many of the homes on the market had old furniture, some of which was not just beautiful but also had real value in the antique business. So, I began buying pieces of furniture, and paintings as well, from the owners when I'd list the houses." He paused to add some cream to the coffee the waiter had just brought "Before I knew it, I found myself in the market of finding old pieces for collectors. Word of mouth brought me commissions to transport furniture between Europe and the U.S. When I discovered Ireland, I decided it was a perfect place to base my operation, then branch out with the newsletter. I wish my Dad could see me now."

"It sounds fascinating," I told him. I pictured myself searching through catalogues and museums trying to figure out the history of a piece of furniture. I imagined the owners, what their life might have been like. Whose hands had polished the piece? Who might have pounded it with a fist? Or slept on it? Or hidden behind it? Fidgeting in my seat, I was suddenly anxious to get back to my computers, databases, and information brokering.

Peter glanced down at his watch. "I have an early appointment tomorrow, and judging from what you've told me about your investigation, you need rest, too. How about I get you home before your carriage turns into a pumpkin and you decide not to have dinner with me again?"

"That sounds reasonable enough," I said, and we both rose from our seats.

That's when I noticed Lorcan sitting with an attractive blonde at one of the other tables in the nave. The woman's luxurious hair swept down toward the middle of her back, and her blue eyes sparkled as she leaned forward to hang on Lorcan's every word. Oddly, I felt a pang of regret, which quickly morphed into full-blown jealousy. Heat surged through my body, flaming my face as I then experienced a feeling of unfaithfulness to Peter and Dylan. Unable to avoid their table as we walked out, I hurried past in the hope that Lorcan wouldn't see me. No such luck.

"Star!" He uncoiled his six-two frame from his chair and grinned down at me. "I'd like you to meet my...."

"Lorcan," I cut him off. "This is Peter Hughes. Peter's a close friend of mine."

I paused to emphasize the word close, studying Lorcan's face for his reaction.

He and Peter stared at each other as if something flashed between them. Lorcan's eyes searched Peter's face for a few uncomfortable moments before he finally offered his hand to Peter.

"You're a lucky man," Lorcan told him. "Star doesn't grant her friendship to many people." Then, addressing both of us, he continued with, "And this is my cousin, Emma. She's visiting my mother for a few days."

After awkward hellos, we exchanged brief words about the restaurant's fine service and whatnot. Then, after what seemed like an eternity, we said our goodnights. I hurried Peter along, telling him I was tired. When we arrived at the gate, Peter stopped the car, walked me to the front door, and said "I'll pick you up on Tuesday morning. Say, eight o'clock?"

I nodded my agreement and offered him my hand. "Thank you for dinner. I had a wonderful..."

I couldn't finish my sentence because he pulled me toward him, then gently brushed his lips over my own.

"Uh, Peter," I began. But he put his finger to my lips.

"Don't say anything," he told me. "I'll see you on Tuesday." Then he was gone.

LATER, I LAY AWAKE IN MY BED STARING AT THE CEILING. AS I touched my own fingers to my lips, thoughts of Peter's warm caress intermingled with images of Dylan's strong and capable arms embracing me. Then, without warning, my mind conjured up Lorcan's face grinning down at me.

Finally, I turned off the light and decided to forget all about men for the night.

CHAPTER 11

T he man with the multi-colored hair stood at the edge of the cliff. *What the hell is he doing? I wondered. He's going to fall! I have to help him! I willed my feet to move faster. But they wouldn't move. Oh, my God, he's falling!* "Help!" *I screamed.* "Somebody help!!!"

My pounding heart startled me awake. Then I realized I was immobilized with crippling fear, my limbs unable to budge. Staring up at the ceiling, my senses absorbed my surroundings while my body recovered from the adrenaline.

A dream, I realized. *It was only a dream.* But reality was even edgier as I acknowledged the fear that I wouldn't be able to deal with what had happened to Matthew while in such a fragile state. I had only just begun my investigation and I was already having nightmares. After all, it hadn't been that long since Dylan had died. Was I ready to relive the pain and memories of one death as I delved into another? Maybe it was time to talk to Bridget about letting go and just accepting the police and the coroner's report.

Then rationality came back to me, and with it the cognizance of how idiotic this notion really was. How could I ask Bridget to let go of this? And all because of a bad dream?

How many times would I dream about Matthew? It's my Gaelic blood, after all. I feel the sorrow and pain of other people's losses. It's made me too damned sensitive and intuitive. My only defense is to leap into action, one foot in front of the other, one step at a time. It's also the only way to beat off the crippling Celtic twilight.

With that image in mind, I rolled over and hit the floor running.

I MADE AN APPOINTMENT TO SEE MATTHEW'S FIANCÉE, SHARON, and she agreed to meet at twelve thirty that afternoon. As I drove toward her address, I noted that her neighborhood shouted money. Multi-story, multi-bedroom brick homes with skylights, lush landscaping, and lengthy, winding, lamp-lit drives were the norm out here. Bold pigments of dark blue, green, red, and black adorned double doors. Glass-enclosed sunrooms, like rigid appendages, attached themselves to each home. Such a stark contrast to the thousands of small cottages with turf fireplaces and a few measly acres out back.

I arrived finally at the Brownsville Flats. They were once a nunnery, but that had been traded in and remodeled into spacious luxury apartments. An elaborate wrought iron gate guarded the enclosure. The royal blue doors suggested richness and superiority.

A black Lexus occupied Sharon's driveway. Aunt Georgina had described her as a diligent and highly regarded financial planner who had once been a stockbroker, working for Merrill Lynch and specializing in technology stocks.

Sharon opened the door, stepping back to allow me in. The high-end furniture and clearly genuine paintings which hung on the foyer walls arrested my eyes. Recognizing a David Hockney, I wondered if her taste in art was the glue that brought her and Matthew together.

"Good, you're on time," she said, but still clearly annoyed. "I have to make calls this afternoon that can't be cancelled. Come in." I immediately felt like an unwanted but necessary repair person who'd ruined her day.

Her voice was cool, low, and without accent. I figured she must have taken lessons to neutralize the brogue. The stereotypical images of Irish women are founded on Maureen O'Hara —tall, red-haired, and blue eyed. In contrast, Sharon was petite, about five-two. Her short jet-black hair, cut in a tapered bob style, accentuated high cheekbones and the raised eyebrows over her brown eyes. With her golden-olive skin, I would have guessed Spanish, not Irish ancestry. She wore a stylish, brown silk long-sleeved blouse tucked into brown pants and flat leather shoes. Every accessory—earrings, watch, ring— accentuated her skin color and her dark eyes, including the puffy circles that underlined them.

I followed her into an immense living room; no vestiges of a nun's solitary cell remained. White fabrics provided the backdrop for pine and oak woods and black leather seating arrangements. An oriental rug drew attention to the hardwood floor. I figured the rent must be astronomical. Sharon pointed to one of the sofas, telling me to take a seat while she went to get us a drink. Oil paintings hung on all four walls. I scrutinized the signatures and found no Matthew Sumner.

I considered the quiet stateliness of the room, then recalled Matthew's own living quarters. How did he and Sharon complement each other as a couple? How did his passions fit into her world? Did she seek excitement with him as an escape from her high-pressured career?

"I hope you like Riesling," she said as she returned. "It's one of my favorites, Trimbach Cuvée, from Alsace." She handed me a glass. Raising hers to her lips, she took a sip, then smiled and asked, "So what can I tell you, Miss O'Brien?"

"First of all," I began, "I want you to know how sorry I am about what happened to Matthew. I lost someone I loved last year as well. And I know that it hurts for a long time."

Her hand shook slightly as she placed her glass on the table beside mine. She tried to smile again, but this time her face didn't cooperate. Her lips trembled and her hands shook even more.

Believing that it's best to tackle the tough questions first, I asked her, "Had you noticed that Matthew seemed distracted lately?"

For a moment, her eyes shot around the room as if she didn't recognize where she was. Then she replied "Not at all. He was totally absorbed with the art project he's been working on." She bowed her head in the general direction of Clare Island.

"Did he ever mention a place called Tranquility House?" I then explained the brochure I'd found in his townhouse.

"Never." She stood and walked over to the large picture window that contemplated a small green garden containing several ivy and rose arbors. Now she had her back to me, which made reading her difficult. "I thought I knew Matthew," she went on. "I realize now that one never knows another person. Not even oneself. Does one?"

She turned and strode back across the room to the sofa.

"Did he experiment with drugs?" I asked. "Is that what you mean about not knowing him?"

After a long silence, she said, "Matthew changed in the last few months. He overpowered me with questions whenever we were together. Asking me about where I'd been, whom I'd seen. He acted needy and dependent. We hadn't seen much of one another lately. Our careers separated us quite often." She paused here to rub her hands together, as if trying to erase something. "I deal with numbers and data, Ms. O'Brien. Cold, precise information upon which I make decisions that affect my clients' lives, not to mention my own. Matthew dealt in feelings and intuition. He was moody and temperamental." She stopped, ran a hand through her hair, then continued. "He could have experimented with drugs. The guards say he did. Why? Maybe money was an issue. Maybe he envisioned that it would make him more creative. I don't know. And I don't care to know. My feelings for Matthew died long before he did. He just didn't know it."

She reached forward to sip her wine but her trembling hands betrayed her. Instead she withdrew them and launched herself out of the sofa instead.

"Now, is that all? I have an important appointment with a client that I can't be late for."

I got up.

"If you remember anything or anyone that can help me understand what happened, please call me," I said.

"Of course," came her curt reply. Mere seconds later I found myself standing on her front steps again.

As she closed the door behind me, her phone rang.

I SAT IN MY CAR FOR A FEW MINUTES, THINKING ABOUT MY collision with this woman. The newspaper accounts pictured a dynamic, beautiful couple. So what had soured the relationship? And why wouldn't she say more?

Frustrated that I'd hit a dead end, I pondered what to do with the rest of the day, as this appointment had certainly ended earlier than I had expected. I decided to drive to Pontoon for a walk on the beach. I always have an extra pair of socks and running shoes in the trunk for these occasions. The fresh air and change of scenery often provide a shift in my perspective on a problem.

As I pulled away from the curb, I noticed Sharon hurrying out her door. She looked worried and absorbed in where she was going; so much so, in fact, that I don't think she saw me sitting there. And if she did, she didn't acknowledge me. Late for her appointment, I supposed.

I again considered her trembling hands as well as the dark circles under her eyes. These were surprising features for someone expected to be cool and collected enough to handle huge financial sums in a highly stressful environment. If she wasn't in love with Matthew anymore, what was flustering her?

The road between Castlebar and Pontoon veered and twisted like a corkscrew. Barren bog land sprinkled with purple heather and chunks of granite deposited by glaciers stretched for miles on either side of a road that was as narrow as a pencil. Nephin Mountain rose moodily in the distance.

Opening the trunk to don my Nikes, I noticed some fishermen in waders standing in the water a few feet from shore. Ready for my workout, lest I disturb them, I selected the path into the forest instead of the beach.

Within a few minutes, the silver firs enveloped me. As the cold, damp air tickled my nose, I wondered about Sharon's mental state. Not knowing what she was like before Matthew's death, I was at a disadvantage in trying to figure her out. But Bridget had noted a distinct change in Sharon's personality. I couldn't help but empathize with the woman. My hands might not shake, but I know how fragile I've felt since Dylan died. Some people deal with grief differently. I choose to hide my feelings inside—maybe Sharon couldn't do that. Or maybe it was true that Sharon knew more about Matthew's death than she let on.

Gathering my jacket around me to retain body heat in the suddenly cool sun-filtered atmosphere, I heard something crackling in the trees to my left. I stopped, scanning the space around me. Nothing but silence. I shrugged, relegated the noise to my imagination, and continued on the circular trail. I soon glimpsed light again as well as the parking lot. Then I picked up speed as the sounds of breaking branches and undergrowth grew louder. I had the impression an eternity passed before I emerged from the woods.

"*Sheba!*" a masculine voice yelled. "*Here girl!*"

An Irish Kerry Blue terrier, its wavy coat matted with twigs and leaves, bounded out of the woods, stopped, took stock of me, and wagged its tail before charging off toward her master's voice.

THE SUN HAD DROPPED BELOW THE HORIZON WHEN I ARRIVED back to find Peter sitting on the stone wall near the front gate.

"I hope you don't mind me dropping by," he said as he held the wrought iron entry open for me. "I thought you might like some company."

"Not at all. How about a cup of tea?"

"I'd love some," he replied.

We headed through the gate and around the side path to the kitchen door. *Drop-in guests....* I couldn't imagine doing anything like this back in Ridgewood. When Dylan and I worked, our schedules left little room for company. And on the rare occasion when we weren't toiling at our respective careers, we selfishly guarded how and with whom we spent our free hours. In contrast, random visits were part of the fabric of Ireland's community and village life. Rare was the afternoon when nobody stopped in for a few minutes to chat about the weather or ask me how long I planned on staying. I'd learned to keep a package of McVities milk chocolate digestive biscuits —"biccies" as the Irish call them—milk, and Lyons original blend tea on hand.

I hadn't expected to see Peter so soon. Was he just practicing one of the country's customs, or was he rushing our relationship? I hoped it wasn't the latter because I needed to get to know him a lot better before I could make a commitment.

"Make yourself at home," I told him as we walked inside. "This'll only take a few minutes."

While I brewed a pot of Lyons for him and heated water for my peppermint tea, he ambled around the living room and admired some of the furniture. For me, the process of making tea—boiling the water, scalding the pot, measuring the leaves into a bag—is as comforting as holding the warm mug in my hands and savoring the brew itself. I even considered the idea of sharing this ritual with Peter.

"I see you've got some antiques here," he said, running his hands over a mahogany side table.

"I suppose," I said, bringing the tea into the room on a tray. "It was a total surprise to me that Dylan even had this place."

"Yes, I remember you mentioned that when we met." He walked over to the mantelpiece and picked up one of the brass candlestick holders, studying the maker's mark. "I never met him, but his import business was well known in my circles. Why wouldn't he mention this house to you?"

"I have no idea, and I haven't given it much thought, either." I placed the tray on the coffee table. "I've been focused on the search for my mother and whether or not to sell this place."

Who was I kidding? This secret of Dylan's was a large meditation of mine but not one that I wanted to discuss.

Taking my cue, Peter said "Well, if you ever decide to sell," Peter said, "let me know. I'll help you appraise the furniture. There are several pieces here that are quite valuable." Then, sinking into one of the wing chairs with tea in hand, he asked, "So I guess you worked on your case today?"

"Yes. I met with Sharon Dawson."

"Really! Did she tell you anything?"

"No. Nothing. It's strange and frustrating," I said. Then I

recited my conversation with her. "And I didn't realize it until just now, but she had nothing of a personal nature in her sitting room. No family pictures, none of Matthew. Judging by the expensive artwork on her walls, she's obviously a collector. But she didn't have any pieces belonging to Matthew."

"That doesn't really mean anything, does it?" he said. "I mean it sounds like she's just a very private person."

"She doesn't seem to be the type of woman that I'd have figured Matthew to have a relationship with," I told him.

Peter twisted his silver bracelet. It seemed like an absent, almost nervous gesture. "Opposites attract. Perhaps her strengths were what he needed and vice versa."

"You're probably right. But I think I'll go back to talk to her again. She was troubled, and I'd like to know what about."

"Well, not tomorrow. We have a date to drive to Dublin, remember? I'll be here bright and early. And plan on having dinner with me tomorrow evening as well. That's an order. I'll be returning to Clare Island on Saturday, and it'll be some time before I'm back on the mainland. I have a new commission to find a pair of eighteenth-century antique earrings that I need to tend to."

He placed his empty cup on the side table, got up, and waited.

I rose and walked him to the door.

"In the morning then," I started to say when he turned and brushed my cheek with his lips. Then he was gone.

I rubbed the cheek in question, which was now burning. The only man I've loved was Dylan. Did the rare brand of true caring that Dylan and I shared happen more than once? Could my feelings of romantic desire and magnetic physical attraction to Peter grow into affection and compassion? I didn't know. But I did wonder if perhaps it was time to put the past to rest and look to the future.

I MOVED INTO THE KITCHEN TO TIDY UP THE DISHES, THEN THE phone intruded on my mission. I guessed it might be Aunt Georgina—but it wasn't.

"Would you be interested in attending a gala black-tie dinner with me?" Lorcan asked. "Healy's Hotel in Pontoon is hosting a charity auction, and I'd be pleased if you were my guest."

I twisted the phone cord in my hand as I considered the invitation. Whatever had given him the idea to call me for a date? And how could I trust someone whom Dylan dismissed with an eye roll?

But before I had a chance to respond, Lorcan's voice vibrated over the telephone line— "My mother is one of the auction's sponsors, and Georgina is supplying some of the prizes. I think you'll enjoy it. It's a fun night and supports a worthwhile cause."

I shook my head as it dawned on me that Aunt Georgina was probably behind this. What could it hurt to go with him? Besides, it didn't sound like I'd be alone with the man. Aunt Georgina would be there, not to mention countless other people.

I could hear his quiet breathing on the other end of the line as he waited. The telephone cord bounced in my hands when I released it. Remembering the news articles I'd come across in the library about Sharon, Raymond, and Matthew, I decided attending the gala might be informative.

"When is it? I'll have to check my calendar." While I waited for his reply, I thought about the emptiness of my calendar.

"Wednesday night." Lorcan said.

"Okay, I'll go." I told him, guessing that Sharon and Raymond's attendance would provide an opportunity to observe them in a more relaxed and open atmosphere.

"Good." Lorcan paused. "Let's see, I'll pick you up at nine. That will give us plenty of time for a leisurely drive to Pontoon before the gala begins at nine thirty. Anyway, I'll talk to you before Wednesday," he said.

Then the line went dead.

CHAPTER 12

"What's the bag for?" I asked Peter as I glided across the seat into his car.

He smiled. "When it's this early in the morning, the Upper Crust's raisin scones are still warm from the oven. I had an idea that you might not make lunch."

"Totally forgot about it," I said, noting the steam escaping from the Styrofoam cups in their holders. I reached for one of them. "You supplied the beverages too. It looks good."

The dregs of tea at the bottom of the cups were cold and the scones were long gone by the time I finished telling Peter about my childhood and how the search for my Mother had led to launching the Consulting Detective.

"Don't you feel like this searching for Mom is useless?" he asked, munching on the last few crumbs of pastry. "I mean there's so much mystery surrounding your mother's family."

"I've dreamed of hugging my mother every day of my life," I said, brushing the last bits of flour from my hands onto a napkin Peter had provided. "Frustration is a small price to pay."

He glanced over at me tentatively. "Shouldn't you be devoting more time, then, hunting down leads? I mean, you've said that you're returning to the States soon. I just think this is your chance to talk to people before you revert to your life back home."

"That's the catch," I replied, exhaling deeply to release my momentary impatience. "Finding people who might have known her or her family. Record and document keeping is more of an oral history than a written one in Ireland. But I'm persistent. And my return to the States is flexible. I don't have relationships which need nurturing." I paused, then added, "At least right now."

"Doesn't your company require you to run it?"

"It's fine. I'm the one who's at loose ends, not being able to walk into my office and get into my world of data." I shot a look at the iPhone, nestled in its case and clipped to my purse, even though it didn't really work on this side of the pond.

"Sometimes when I'm on the prowl for old furniture," Peter went on, "I write about it in my newsletter, and often someone will contact me with a lead. Have you tried any of the online newsletters or chat rooms?"

"Incessantly, but with no result," I said. "Although I've been successful with searches for other people. I located someone's cousin on a surname community board. The woman just happened to have posted there, and one of my software programs found the reference." Picturing the family reunion that my client likely enjoyed afterward, I stifled a tear.

As Peter turned onto one of the quays along the Liffey river, he reached over and took hold of my hand. "Well, please let me know if I can help," he said gently.

He parked as close as he could get to Dublin Castle. He planned on taking the guided tour to look at some of the antiques, then meet up with his client for lunch. We agreed to rendezvous at Bewley's Café—one of Dublin's oldest landmarks, in the heart of Grafton Street, serving up the best coffee and chocolates imaginable—at 4:00 p.m.

I hadn't told Peter that I intended to visit the General Register Office after my interview at Tranquility House. I remembered the negative responses I'd received when I'd called and written the office—

No, we don't research family history....

No, we don't have an online index....

Sorry, but it's first-come first-served if you wish to visit the Research Room....

—so, needless to say, I longed to make an in-person plea and go through the files myself.

The brochure for Tranquility House listed a Heuston Street address. A guard near the castle gates provided directions, recommending a cab after he explained that it was a thirty-minute walk. Impatient for action, I opted for the walk. I picked up speed, mingling with the sea of bobbing heads on the crowded sidewalks as people hurried along, reminding me of New York's Fifth Avenue.

At that moment, a wave of homesickness pummeled me. How long would it be before I returned to New Jersey? To my dog, my house, and my friends? *Soon*, I promised myself, knowing it was a promise I might not keep.

Tranquility House turned out to be a three-story brick structure. True to Dublin's Georgian door fashion, it sported a green portal. I rang the bell and waited for a response. A tall blonde woman escorted me into a spacious office.

"Would you like anything to drink, Miss O'Brien?" she asked.

"No, thank you. Is Ms. Burns expecting me?"

"Yes, she'll be here in a few minutes. Please make yourself comfortable." She did not close the door when she left the room, which prohibited me from snooping. Instead I crossed over to the picture window and watched the double decker buses transporting people to and from the Heuston Street station.

Ten minutes later, Mary Alice Burns swept into the room. She wore a fuchsia-colored suit with gold accessories. Black hair was molded into a pageboy that she wore like a helmet. She marched toward me with her hand outstretched. Her handshake was firm and quick.

"I hope you weren't waiting too long, Ms. O'Brien. I'm burning the candle at both ends today. Please sit down." She strode around her desk and sat down as she indicated a chair to me.

I decided to come to the point immediately.

"Ms. Burns, I'm investigating Matthew Sumner's death," I said. Then I paused to allow for her reaction. When there was none, I continued, "I have information that he met with you shortly before his death. I want to know what you discussed." I eased back in my chair and waited.

"Matthew's sister called me, so I know what she's asked you to do," she replied. "I must say that I don't envy you your job. Cases like these are never resolved for the people who are left behind. Bridget Sumner is experiencing the denial stage of the grief process. It's very similar to what people with dependencies and their families live through. But time heals all, and she'll see that eventually." She paused to use her long-manicured fingernails to tap the files on her desk into a straight line. "Of course, I'll tell you about the meeting, although there isn't much to report. Matthew required information about our drug rehabilitation program, specifically the resident-recovery process. I gave it to him and then he left. It's as simple as that."

"Did he indicate why he needed the information? Did he say that it was for him?"

"He didn't reveal who the candidate was, if that's what you mean, which is normal in situations where there's a drug dependency. People don't want to admit their vulnerabilities or those of their family during the early steps toward intervention. He was adamant about our ability to protect residents' identities. He asked questions about access to the program's participants, visitors' rights, and so on." She pushed the files around until they needed to be straightened again. "He also wanted to know when the next opening for a resident would be."

"What did you tell him?" I was curious to know the timing and how it might connect to his death.

"September. Several of our current residents transition from here back to their home environment that month. Matthew became anxious, almost panicked when he heard this. He pressured me to do something about finding space sooner."

"Was that a typical response in a case like this?"

"Yes and no." Tilting her head toward the file folders, she explained— "Most often families want to get the process started. They worry about what might happen to the candidate before he or she enters the program. In comparison to the urgency I usually deal with on behalf of families in this situation, Matthew's reaction was explosive. He said that money was no object. I tried to explain that it was more than money, that there's quite a bit of preparation involved. When he finally realized that it was September or nothing, he stormed out, slamming the door. His behavior was rude and inappropriate." She sat back then, waiting for me to speak.

"Do you think he was the candidate?"

She leaned forward and gazed directly into my eyes, "I'm a licensed professional therapist and counselor. I wouldn't think of venturing any opinion of that nature without having conducted an investigation and analysis of the client first. Matthew didn't give me that opportunity." Then she propelled herself away from her desk. "I don't have any more to tell you, Ms. O'Brien. If you don't mind, I have a practice to run." She strode around the desk and motioned me to precede her through the door.

Back outside, I replayed the meeting in my head and considered the implications. Our discussion confirmed that Matthew's recent activities before his death were related to drugs. What exactly the relationship was, I didn't know yet. But the timing of his demise, coming on the heels of his visit to Dublin, solidified my belief that his death had not been an accidental stumble from a cliff.

I glanced at my watch. Two hours remained before I was scheduled to meet Peter. Plenty of time to get to the General Register Office. I tugged a city street map out of my jacket pocket and located the address on Lombard Street. If I power walked, I'd arrive in twenty minutes. So, sprinting down the steps of Tranquility House, I broke out into a heel-to-toe lilt across the intersection of Heuston and Gloucester Streets.

CHAPTER 13

P eople bustled all around me, moving with purpose as they scurried to catch taxis, buses, and trains. Pausing to regain my balance as the result of a bump from behind, my heart thumped erratically when my eyes focused on a woman who was crossing the street in front of me. I hastened to get abreast of her—to look at her face. The woman's walk, the way she moved, childhood images of me trailing behind my mother exploded in my brain. Could it be her?

Halfway across the avenue, I became aware of urgent shouts over the roar of an engine. Twisting to my right, I spotted a black car hurtling at me like a bullet train. I froze at first, gaping at the oncoming vehicle while expecting it to slow down. Instead, it kept rocketing in my direction. Then I dove for the sidewalk, reaching it by a narrow margin and feeling the rush of air whistle past while the car zoomed by.

Face down in the gutter, I was soon aware of a dozen pairs of shoes surrounding me. A hand reached down and pulled me into a sitting position. I gazed up hopefully, seeking the face on the other end. Needless to say, I was crushed to find a stranger staring down at me.

Blood gushed from my left hand. My trouser legs felt wet,

and I peered down to find rivulets of blood trickling onto my ankles. I soon discovered two badly scraped knees. *At least all the body parts are still attached*, I thought morbidly. I tapped my nose to be sure, because it ached like hell. Several other people attached to the shoes helped me stand up, then escorted me to a nearby walk-in urgent-care clinic.

OF COURSE, THE WOMAN I'D SEEN ON THE STREET WAS LONG gone. Had it been my mother? It was a possibility. I've located someone's long lost relative dozens of times living only a few miles from their family. They'd be residing in familiar surroundings and yet lost in the crowd of a big city or town. It often came down to circumstances. Maybe my mom had been in an accident the day she disappeared. Maybe she had amnesia and didn't remember she'd had a child. Maybe she'd gone on an errand and had been hit by a car. I'd checked all the local hospital and police records for accidents, with no luck. But that didn't mean it hadn't happened. The paperwork could have been misfiled.

All of these possibilities occupied my mind while a curly-haired, brown-eyed nurse checked me over, cleaned me up, and wrapped me in bandages. Nothing was broken, but I had some nasty cuts and bruises on my face, hands, and knees.

"Look both ways before you cross the road next time, Miss O'Brien," he said as he handed me a copy of the medical report and my bill. "Dublin streets are dangerous thoroughfares."

Thanking him for his efforts, I hobbled back onto the sidewalk. It was almost four o'clock now; time to meet Peter. So much for personal research, I reflected as I crawled into the back of a cab that dropped me at the corner of Grafton and Nassau streets. Like a tortoise, I crept along the cobblestones trying to avoid being jostled by the throngs of students, shoppers, and tourists surging through the city center while getting to where Peter was stationed outside the famous café.

His smile crumbled when he finally saw me.

"What happened?" he asked as he wrapped his arm around my shoulders and guided me toward the rear of the restaurant's cavernous dining room. He moved furniture out of the way and gently helped me sit down in a booth.

"Now tell me what happened," he said, taking the opposite seat and holding my hands.

"Peter, please. Don't make a big deal of this," I responded, pulling my hands back. "It was nothing."

"Nothing?!" his voice rose above the restaurant's din, causing the people sitting closest to us to stare. "You look like you've been in an accident! Tell me what happened, now!"

"I had a close encounter with the sidewalk. I was crossing the street when a car came out of nowhere and almost ran me over." I shivered, remembering the image of the vehicle bearing down upon me and the *whoosh* of the vehicle's engine rushing toward me. "I could really use a cup of herbal tea right now."

"Wait here. I'll go get it. Peppermint, right?"

I nodded and rested my head against the back of the booth. Peter strode to the restaurant's café section to stand in line and place the order. I used the few minutes alone to close my eyes and ignore the gawkers around me.

He was back within fifteen minutes, and soon I felt more like my old self. A crumpled napkin laid on the table. My tea cup was empty.

"It was probably my fault," I said. "It's easy to get confused by the left-hand side driving. Maybe I didn't look in the right direction when I started to cross the street."

He grunted. "You don't seem like the kind of person who'd get confused about traffic. I think it was more than that."

"What's that supposed to mean? What else could it have been?"

"You're asking a lot of people a lot of questions about someone who died under mysterious circumstances. It doesn't take a rocket scientist to understand that if there's something more to this than an accidental slip from a cliff, then playing Nancy Drew just might get you killed. Maybe you should leave it alone."

Although my mood had lightened with the peppermint tea, Peter's had gotten darker. Maybe this idea of traveling together to Dublin had been a bad one. I didn't need negative people around me.

"You know what? This is no place for you to be," He said as his eyes scanned the restaurant. "You need to get home. But there's one thing I want to do before we leave."

"What's that?" I asked. The only thing I longed for at the moment was a warm bath and a hot water bottle. My knees ached as I made a move to stand up.

"Stay there," Peter commanded. "I'll be right back."

I slumped back in the booth and closed my eyes again. I think I was asleep within seconds. When I felt a hand tap my shoulder, I was instantly awake.

"Okay, let's go," Peter said. He reached out his hand to help me up.

"I can get up under my own steam," I told him as I moved my disparate bag of bones from the booth. "So where were you?"

"I spoke with the guards."

I couldn't believe what I was hearing. "The police?!"

"Star, you were the victim of a hit-and-run accident. It should have been reported when it happened. There's nothing they can do anyway now, only make note of what I told them."

"I was the victim of my own carelessness," I retorted and limped toward the door.

I waited in front of Bewley's while Peter went for his car. It was five thirty now and the street surged with the evening tide of workers. When I realized enough time had passed to let Peter get to the car, I began limping toward the Dublin Fusiliers' Arch where he planned to pick me up.

When Raymond Nolan showed up instead, I almost didn't recognize him because he wore a black stocking cap over his blond hair. Another moment and he would have passed me by. Serendipity, I guess. Our eyes locked and surprise registered in his. I stepped into his path.

"Mr. Nolan," I smiled.

"Miss O'Brien. I never expected to find you in Dublin. Seeing the sights, I expect."

It struck me that he appeared to look everywhere but at me. I moved in closer.

"Business, Mr. Nolan. Matthew Summer's business. And you?"

"Business as well. Now if you'll excuse me, I must be getting on." He nodded and drifted away into the crowd.

I found it interesting that he hadn't mentioned my bandages or bruises.

∾

WHEN PETER AND I ARRIVED AT FRENCH HILL COTTAGE, I FELT AS though I'd been away for a week.

"Aunt Georgina's car is here," I noted. "I wonder why? She knew we went to Dublin today."

At that moment, she burst through the brown teak double front door of the cottage, running along the footpath, her scarf billowing behind her. Lorcan trailed her close.

"Oh, I called your aunt after I called the guards," Peter said as he leaned around me and opened the gate.

"Great, just what I needed," I said under my breath. "A welcoming committee with Lorcan on it."

Aunt Georgina inserted herself between Peter and me.

"Star! My God, what happened to you? Come along; you need to get right into the tub!"

"Will the welcoming committee be there too?" I asked.

I regretted my comment immediately. I could understand her reaching out to someone she knew; after all, she didn't know Peter.

Her puzzled look told me she hadn't gotten my joke. "What's that, dear?"

"Nothing, Aunt Georgina. Actually, some food would be nice." I smiled at her, continued past Lorcan, entered the living room, and plunked myself into the love seat that faced the fireplace.

"You look like you're cold." Lorcan said as he draped his brown leather jacket over my shoulders. He and Peter nodded at each other and poured their long frames into the wing chairs.

Fifteen minutes later, everyone took deep gulps from steaming mugs of tea and ate cheese sandwiches courtesy of Aunt Georgina while I explained my cuts and bruises.

Lorcan's eyes were solemn and unsmiling as he pushed his glasses into place and stared at my nose. "Are you sure it was an accident?"

"Of course I'm sure. Either the driver or I—or both of us— were just careless." I shrugged and struggled to get up. "Now if everyone will excuse me, I'd like to call it a night."

"I guess we won't see you speed walking along Cottage Road anytime soon." Lorcan commented as he rose to his feet and shook hands with Peter.

"Don't be too sure of that," I shot back. "It takes more than a fall to keep me down."

"Call me when you're up to it," Peter said as he made his way out of the room.

While Aunt Georgina shuffled Lorcan and Peter out the door (with assurances that she'd take good care of me), I filled the tub and climbed in with my notes about the case. After I finished documenting my visit to Tranquility House, I dropped the notes onto the floor.

Everything I'd learned so far seemed to point toward there being more to Matthew's death than an accident. What I knew for certain was that he was a talented artist with a potentially steady career in front of him. He'd been concerned enough about someone in his life to make the trip to Tranquility House in Dublin. The closest people to him were his longtime friend, Nolan, and his sophisticated and wealthy fiancée Sharon. It seemed strange to me that these two people seemed ready to abandon him in death. Jeez, neither of them appeared to care about what had happened to him and why. I lay prone in the water up to my chin and closed my eyes. But then I could see the black car barreling toward me, so I opened them again.

Grudgingly, I had to admit that it might not have been care- lessness after all.

CHAPTER 14

S ome time later, Lorcan's red-and-white Piper Super Cub's droning engine woke me.

The sun shone steadily around the window shades. I hugged the silk sheets and planted my feet on the still-warm water bottle that Aunt Georgina had fixed the night before. My fingers explored my face and knees for swelling but only found some soreness. Closing my eyes, I willed myself to let the airplane's white noise lull me back to sleep. Thinking about yesterday's events could wait another few hours.

When I raised my lids again, I heard vehicles speeding along cottage road. Reaching under my pillow, I pulled out my watch—just a few minutes after ten o'clock. At that moment, there was a tap on my door and Aunt Georgina glided into the room toting a tray.

I pushed myself up against the headboard, sitting up and slipping on the silk nightshirt I'd taken off during the night when the warmth of the room and bed had combined to make me feel like a sun-dried raisin.

"Aunt Georgina," I said, "I didn't hear you come in."

"I came through the back door. And I've made you breakfast." She placed a tray next to me on the bed.

"Thank you, I'm starving," I said as the aroma of peppermint tea filled my nostrils. While I thoroughly enjoyed the fresh made brown bread, eggs, and bacon she'd conjured up, I managed to tell her that I'd slept through most of the night.

Then I asked, "Where did you get this food? It didn't come from my refrigerator." Only yogurt, fruit, and vegetables occupy my cold space.

"I knew you wouldn't have anything good in this house," she said as she lifted her eyes over her glasses and pointed her finger at me. "I stopped at Quinn's Shop on the way out from town for the bacon and eggs. I made the brown bread myself."

"It's delicious. Is there any more?"

"You can have more after you've gotten up. I'll see you in the kitchen." She scooped up the empty tray and swept out of the room.

She was right—it was time to get up.

First a shower. Padding from my bedroom through the living room, I caught the clatter of the mail slot announcing that the post had arrived. Pivoting around, I saw the scatter of envelopes lying on the rug inside the front door. I left it there and went into the bathroom. Then I was standing under the warm spray until nothing from yesterday remained.

Thirty minutes later I joined Aunt Georgina in the kitchen for another cup of peppermint tea. She had been good enough to retrieve the mail and pile it in the middle of the oak kitchen table.

"How about more of that bread?" I asked as I opened a long envelope that had no return address.

"Of course, there's plenty of it here."

Then I gasped, and Aunt Georgina wheeled around. She dropped the bread knife on the cutting board and moved over to where I stood staring at a single piece of paper.

"What is it, Star?" she said, peeking over my shoulder.

I showed her the one line that was written there, with a magic marker in large block letters—

MIND YOUR BUSINESS YANK,
OR YOU WILL BE SORRY

"Jesus, Mary, and Joseph," she said as her usually dark complexion paled several shades. "Who could have done this?"

The writing on the envelope had also been printed with a black marker. A Castlebar postmark indicated that it had been mailed yesterday morning.

"I have no idea."

I didn't want Aunt Georgina to know how shaken I was by the note, so I folded it calmly and set it aside. In my mind, I could still clearly hear the roar of the car that had tried to run me down yesterday. There was virtually no remaining doubt that yesterday's events had been intentional. I'd obviously come too close for comfort for someone. So how close was I? And to whom?

Georgina wrung her hands. "Maybe it's time to tell Bridget that you've done all you can. After all, you were almost killed yesterday. And now this." She grasped my hand. "Please, Star, listen to me this one time. Please."

"Quit? Why? I'm on to something or I wouldn't have gotten this note. Don't you see? There's no going back now. First the car. Now the note. It's clear that there's more to Matthew's death than the police have made of it. And now I'm in danger. That's even more reason to find who's responsible. If I don't, maybe I'll end up the same as Matthew."

Before she had a change to argue, I kissed her cheek and then reached for the phone.

"Okay, so what do you plan to do?" Aunt Georgina asked as she poured herself another cup of tea.

"First, I'm going to lug these aching bones on a power walk," I told her. "Then I intend to talk with Raymond Nolan."

"SAVE THE PEOPLE," SAID THE VOICE AT THE OTHER END OF THE line. "How may I direct your call?"

"Raymond Nolan, please."

"I'm sorry, Mr. Nolan was delayed in traffic coming down from Dublin. We're expecting him back after one o'clock. May I take a message?"

"This is Star O'Brien. Mr. Nolan told me that he'd meet with me at two, so I'm calling to confirm." I relied on the fact that by the time Nolan's secretary learned that we didn't have an appointment; I'd already be sitting in his office waiting room.

"No problem," she said. "See you at two, Miss O'Brien."

"Oh, and I'm curious," I said before she rang off. "What kind of car does Mr. Nolan drive? I'm planning on commuting between here and Dublin and I'm wondering what might be best to buy." I didn't know if his assistant would bite on this bait but it was worth a try.

"He drives a Mercedes. I think he bought it recently. I'm sure he'd be willing to talk more about it with you when you're here."

"Okay, thanks," I said, "See you later."

I saw Aunt Georgina looking thoughtful when I went to get my sneakers.

"I'm sure that if you called him, Lorcan would go with you this afternoon."

"No way," I retorted. "I don't need anybody."

"But Star, don't you think you should let the guards know about the letter?

"I appreciate your concern, Aunt Georgina. But don't you see that I have to do this alone. I have to take care of myself."

Her big brown eyes glistened with tears as I walked over and hugged her.

"I love you and I know you love me," I went on. "And I promise to take care of myself. The police are incompetent most of the time anyway. If they'd done their job, things wouldn't have gotten this far. I do wish I had some of my contacts from Ridgewood here with me, but since I don't.... Well, I'd better go for my walk."

I gave Georgina one last hug, then went and changed into my exercise gear. When I returned, she'd vanished. But there was a note—

Had to dash off to keep an appointment, darling. Have you really considered confiding in Lorcan? Bringing him up to date on any suspicions you might have? Just a thought. Be careful and call me to let me know what you're doing and where you're going. And please don't do anything foolish.

Love, Georgina.

P.S. Don't forget the gala tonight. Wear the maroon dress.

I smiled at the fact that she underlined 'Love.' Aunt Georgina was a treasure.

LEAVING HER NOTE ON THE TABLE, I HEADED OUT FOR MY WALK. I hadn't gone far when I spotted Lorcan speaking with some of the neighboring farmers. I remembered hearing his plane this morning. And it made me wonder how he seemed to materialize at my weakest moments. If last night wasn't enough, now he had to see me moving like an arthritic crab.

"Good morning!" I called to the group at large. "Beautiful day, isn't it?"

The farmers lifted their caps and raised their hands in greeting. Then Lorcan broke away to join me.

"Hey, I'm glad to see you're feeling better," he said.

"Thanks, I'll be okay. So, what are you doing with the local farmers? You're not around here very often. I imagined you spend most of your time pursuing loftier goals in your airplane. Speaking of which, didn't I hear your winged bird flying overhead this morning?"

Lorcan paused and studied the papers in his hand before answering.

"Yes, you did. I took off to check the weather conditions, but the ceilings were too low for visual flight so I changed my mind about the trip. As for the rest of your questions, you haven't been here long enough to know much about what I do." His fingers played with the edges of the paper. "The local farmers and I have created a new water scheme for the area."

"Water? I'd have thought the climate provided all the water the farmers needed."

"It may appear that it rains all the time, but we do have our droughts. Last year's was a doozy, and many of the livestock—not to mention the farmers themselves—suffered from the intense heat and lack of water." He tapped to his papers with one finger. "So I've created a device that will bring water from some of the local lakes to the farms."

"Oh, that sounds useful," I said, although I hated to admit it.

"Well, let me know if I can help with anything." Lorcan looked down at his papers again before continuing. "With the accident yesterday, I was wondering if you're still planning on attending the gala tonight?" His blue eyes caught mine directly at that moment.

I busied my hands by pushing my sleeves up to my elbows

and adjusting my sunglasses while I considered my options. I reminded myself that I had made a commitment. Plus I didn't want to disappoint Aunt Georgina.

"I'm going," I told him, "but I may want to leave early. I'm not much of a night person, and I have a busy day tomorrow."

"We can leave the event early if you want," he replied. "It's only a short ride from here to Pontoon. And my mother will be happy to hear that you're on the move. She was worried, and it will do her good to see you in person." He gently squeezed my elbow and redirected his attention back to the men. Now it was my turn to be surprised. I hadn't expected this gentle kindness from him.

On the way back from my walk, Anne Sullivan—one of my neighbors—waved me over to her gate.

"I picked some flowers for you," she said, offering a large bouquet of roses, zinnias, daisies, and daffodils from her garden.

"Well, thank you very much," I said as I took hold of them. Admiring the vibrant yellows, oranges, and reds, I buried my nose in their fragrance. "They're beautiful!"

"I always gave Dylan flowers when he was on holiday," she said. "That was a long time ago. I miss his visits. It's nice to see a light in his cottage again at night. Will you be staying long?" Then she quickly added, "Wouldn't it be nice if you *stayed* in Ireland?"

For a moment I felt emotionally ripped apart—torn between the beauty of this country and my own ties back in New Jersey. I was divided by two uncontrollable forces—needing to know my mother, but wanting to live my own life. Why hadn't Dylan told me about this place? Why hadn't we journeyed here together on my quest? When had he visited? And why?

I shook my head to jar these notions from my mind. I already had enough to take care of without letting Dylan's secrets use up more space. I'd deal with that later. Besides, whatever his reasons were, I'm sure they had been out of love for me. Of that I was certain.

"Thank you, Mrs. Sullivan," I said. "I'll stop up one evening to visit you before I leave." Then I touched her hand before continuing back to the cottage.

When I opened the door, I saw that the answering machine light was blinking. *Oh, oh, Raymond Nolan's office*, I thought to myself. But when it hit the button, Peter's voice asked how I felt and said that he'd call me later. I smiled when I realized that I looked forward to it.

I ARRIVED AT NOLAN'S OFFICE AT ONE O'CLOCK BECAUSE I WASN'T taking any chances. While I waited, I wondered about Nolan's motives and feelings regarding Matthew. From what Aunt Georgina had said and what I had gleaned from the newspapers in the library, Sharon, Raymond, and Matthew spent a lot of time together, between working at the foundation and attending social functions. So what happened between them to turn Nolan surly whenever he spoke about Matthew?

Raymond Nolan wasn't happy to see me when his assistant escorted me to his office door.

"Miss O'Brien, this way," he said in a tone of voice terse enough to sound like Morse code. He opened the door and then turned his back while I tracked him into his inner sanctum. He pointed to a visitor's chair and then lowered himself into the one at his desk.

"What now, Miss O'Brien? I'm busy this afternoon. I've been out of the office and I have a lot of messages to return." I couldn't help noticing that he never mentioned my cuts and bruises, although I caught him perusing my knees.

"Don't you want to know how I got these injuries?"

"I don't give a damn how you got them. Dublin can be a dangerous place. Maybe you should return to where you came from."

"That's interesting. I never mentioned Dublin. What makes you think that's where this happened?"

"I'm not stupid Miss O'Brien. Inasmuch as I don't really want to have anything to do with you, it was fairly obvious to me when I saw you yesterday that something had happened. I just assumed it happened in the city, that's all."

Surprised by his acknowledgement, I continued with my purpose for the visit.

"I want access to Matthew's files," I said, looking him straight in the eye. I knew getting the files was an unlikely possibility but I'd make my best effort.

"You want access to his private files?" he asked. His eyes bulged as his face flushed scarlet.

"Yes," I replied without hesitation. "I've been to Tranquility House in Dublin. Matthew was there a few days before he died. He inquired about the resident dependency program. The files may provide a clue about who he planned to admit there. His interest in the program must be related to his death."

"Of course, it's related. Have you ever considered that he may have had a drug problem? That the interest in Tranquility House was for himself?" He pounded the desk to punctuate his statement.

"There's no indication that Matthew was a user. The drugs found on the body were in his pants." I continued to hold his eyes with mine. "I know the report says his blood stream contained trace amounts, but nothing in the way he lived his life coincides with that finding.

"No indication that a Yank who doesn't know the local people or how things are done around here would see," he shot back as he continued pounding on the desk. "Just who do you think you are, nosing about into other people's business?"

"Is there something you want to tell me that will enlighten me?"

"I don't believe anyone could enlighten you, Miss O'Brien. Perhaps you want more people to die and then you'll be satisfied. I won't give you his files." The desk experienced one last thump before he jumped up and began pacing back and forth behind it.

"So you do know something," I said as an anger matching his began erupting inside. "Maybe *you're* the one who had something to do with his murder? Just how innocent are you in all of this? And who else do you think might die? Me? Are you threatening me? Someone tried to run me down yesterday in Dublin. Who will testify to your activities and whereabouts yesterday?"

This outburst may have surprised me more than it did Nolan. I was Star O'Brien, and I didn't admit fear to anyone. Was my anger directed at the person who had almost hit me, or at the woman I'd imagined was my mother?

When I finished speaking, he stopped pacing and plopped down again behind his desk.

"I won't give you the files. They are private," he said flatly. Then he attacked the desk with his hand again. "I'm telling you Matthew was dirty. I saw him with Allen Skye. There can only be one reason for that."

"Like what? And who's Allen Skye?"

"I'm surprised you don't know him. Dylan Hill did. Weren't you Hill's fiancée?"

I stopped breathing. Nolan's words slammed into me as if he'd crashed a fist into my heart. *How many secrets did Dylan have?* I couldn't help wondering. Meanwhile, Nolan continued talking through my silence.

"Allen Skye is a known drug dealer who targets children. He's too slippery for the guards to pin anything on him. I've come across him several times in the past two years when I've been working with some of the teenagers who are in our program." Nolan paused, rubbed the hand he'd been using to hammer the desk, and then continued. "Matthew knew him. I saw the two of them recently at the Wagon Wheel pub. They had a fight. And they didn't like it when they caught me observing them."

I began getting excited—this could be the information I needed to find out what troubled Matthew before his death.

"Did you overhear anything?" I asked. "Did they say anything to you?"

"They took off as soon as they realized I'd spotted them. That's all I can tell you. No decent person could spend any time in that vermin Skye's company. Matthew must have been mixed up in something—something that he didn't tell me about. Now, please don't waste any more of my time," he said, scowling at me as he thrust himself out of his chair.

"Thanks." I smiled at him and carried myself as well as my dignity back outside.

I SPENT A FEW MINUTES WALKING AROUND TOWN TO LOCATE THE Wagon Wheel pub, but with no luck. Confident that I could find it at a later date, I went back to French Hill cottage and fell into bed for some troubled sleep. Later, I woke to the sound of a light rain and lay there listening until it was time to get ready for the gala.

Wear the maroon dress.... Aunt Georgina's words lingered in my ears as I draped the silk material over my head, smoothed my hair in place, and donned my heels. Forty minutes later, Lorcan parked his hybrid SUV in Healy's carpark and escorted me into the brightly lit ballroom.

Chandeliers rained droplets of light that bounced back from Waterford crystal vases and lanterns tucked into corner nooks, mantelpieces, and serving tables throughout the room. An indecipherable mix of music and voices ebbed and flowed like the servers who silently floated through the room offering sparkling wine and hors d'oeuvres. For the moment, any thoughts of finding Sharon or Raymond in the crowd were spoiled by the overwhelming rush of people who came to speak with Lorcan when we arrived. He kept his arm casually draped around my shoulders as he exchanged pleasantries and introduced me to everyone.

Strange, isn't it? I'd never have guessed at how popular Lorcan seemed to be. The litany of cordial welcomes and invitations streamed as freely as the champagne. Before long, I felt as if I'd always been part of this community.

As the flow of newcomers entering the room forced us to move further inside, I spotted Aunt Georgina and Lorcan's mother at one of the tables. They were busy arranging the auction items—outdoor grills, Waterford Crystal, lamps, jewelry, golf shoes, vacation tickets to continental Europe, and framed paintings. Excusing myself, I made my way over there.

"I'm so happy you were able to join us!" Lady Marcella said, squeezing my shoulder and smiling. "Lorcan told me about your unfortunate accident in Dublin," She said. Then she leaned closer to me before continuing in a hushed tone, "And, you're not the only one. Sharon mentioned that something similar happened to her in Dublin this week. No wonder she's so peckish lately." Lady Marcella was then interrupted by someone heaping praises concerning the event. "Excuse me, Star," she said a moment later, "I see the manager over there and I want to ask him for another table." Then she waved at a figure across the room and glided away.

Aunt Georgina was continuing to tidy more of the prizes while Lorcan showed up with two glasses of champagne in his hands.

"I hope you like this" he said as he handed one to me.

"Thank you," I replied, not wanting to explain that I don't drink alcohol. But on a positive note, the glass gave me something to do with my hands other than attack my phone while I looked around the room for signs of Raymond or Sharon.

"Have you ever been to a fund-raising auction?" Lorcan asked as he picked a bacon- wrapped scallop from the tray offered by one of the servers.

"No, I'm usually too busy with my business." I thought for a minute before explaining further. "In the work I do, socializing and business don't mix well. Some of the people who employ me wouldn't want to bump into me at a social function." Looking around, I continued with, "Speaking of which, have you seen Raymond or Sharon?"

"No." Lorcan's eyes surveyed the crowded room as if to confirm his answer.

My eyes followed his, and for just a moment I thought I spotted Peter across the room. I wondered why he hadn't mentioned the gala.

"Is that Peter Hughes over there by the door?" I asked.

Lorcan raised his eyebrows, turned to observe the door and then mouthed the word "No" just as the loudspeaker boomed to life and the auction began. The crowd pressed together to focus on the auctioneer, and I lost sight of the man I'd thought was Peter.

The evening's business took off like a rocket, and soon all efforts at conversation stopped as people began bidding and showing off what they'd won. My disappointment at not seeing Raymond or Sharon was short-lived because I got caught up in the excitement radiating throughout the room.

Hours later I found myself holding a 1937 edition of *On Another Man's Wound* by Ernie O'Malley. It was about Ireland's turbulent fight for independence from the English, and I'd won it for just 150 euros. Lorcan, meanwhile, had acquired an old set of surveying tools that he proudly displayed to everyone, commenting that they'd be a great addition to his workshop.

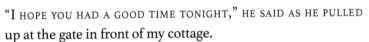

"I HOPE YOU HAD A GOOD TIME TONIGHT," HE SAID AS HE PULLED up at the gate in front of my cottage.

Surprisingly, I had to admit to myself that I did. I really enjoyed the gala's atmosphere of camaraderie and chatter to support a fine cause.

"You were right," I told him, "it was fun. Thank you for including me."

He smiled, his blue eyes twinkling. I wondered what I'd do if he tried to kiss me. But it didn't happen. Instead, he got out of the car, offered his hand as I climbed from the passenger side, and escorted me to the back door.

"Good night, Star. Sleep tight," was all he said. After he drove away, I stood in the kitchen for a few minutes, watching the lights of his car pick their way up the drive to the McHale estate.

I also wondered about his and Dylan's curious relationship.

CHAPTER 15

No surprise that the owners of the Wagon Wheel pub had chosen a country and western theme. Red wheels were fastened to the front of the pub's facade, which faced Lucan Street. A moose's rack of horns guarded the entrance. The antlers must have come from the States because Irish elk are extinct. But that's where the illusion of the Wild West and wide-open spaces ended. Bending myself under the lintel, I sensed I was about to become Gulliver in the country of Lilliput. Anyone over five two or three wouldn't clear the opening without stooping at the waist.

Inside, "Your Cheatin' Heart" by Daniel O'Donnell played in the background to accompany the litany of voices emanating from the bar. Cigarette smoke created a blue veil, through which I saw that most of the people at the bar were men. A few women lounged off to the left, where some benches were scattered around snack tables. I headed in that direction, hoping for one of the available places in the farthest corner of the room. The door and the bar were both visible from that vantage point.

"What would you like to drink, Miss?" asked the dark haired, freckled waitress as she handed me a snack menu.

I smiled at her. "Bottled Ballygowan water with lime will be fine."

"We've got a great selection of draught American beers," she said, pointing to the keg fonts behind the counter.

"Thank you but I'm not a beer drinker." I smiled again as she nodded and circled away.

Perusing the menu, my mouth watered for the chips—thick French fries made from powdery Irish potatoes. The barbecued ribs intrigued me too, as I hypothesized whether an Irish pub could improve on the mesquite ribs I'd had once in Colorado. I ordered them and the chips along with a bowl of vegetable soup.

While I drank my water and waited for my food, I watched the people around me and caught snatches of conversation. Bits and pieces of chatter about concerts, computers, the Internet, and the information age floated back to me. Judging from the discussions, almost everyone here had a technology or computer job. Was Allen Skye one of the men clustered around the bar? If so, perhaps he worked at one of the multinational computer companies in the area. Did he deal at work? I couldn't help wondering. Then again, did he work at all? Or did he make all his money through peddling drugs to children?

In her efforts to educate me, Aunt Georgina said that similar social and economic groups associated with specific pubs in town. All the doctors and nurses went to the Harp Bar, for example, while the farmers went to McCarthy's. I couldn't help but reflect upon where I would fit in if I remained in Ireland.

The waitress appeared with my food, and all thoughts of Allen Skye and the social register of Castlebar faded away. The ribs, meaty and gooey with barbecue sauce, tasted heavenly. Eating them reminded me of the trip that Dylan and I had taken to Durango, Colorado. We rode the steam train to a small mining town called Silverton, up in the mountains. It had taken four hours for the train to climb up through the aspen trees and over the gorges and rivers. Starving when we arrived, we headed for the first barbecue restaurant that we saw. We ate ribs and laughed at each other, our hands and faces becoming incredibly messy with sauce.

The picture melted away. I missed the States and the home that Dylan and I had shared for five years. It belonged to me now. Me alone.

The waitress came back, ready to take my plate. "Can I get you anything else? Is everything okay?"

"No, I'm fine, thank you. But there is something else you might be able to help me with. I'm looking for Allen Skye. I was told that he frequents this pub. Do you know him?"

She froze when she heard the name. Then her eyes opened wide, as she brought them up to meet mine. "Allen Skye, no, can't say that I do now," she replied, snatching up the dishes and moving back over to the bar, where she had a conversation with the bartender.

Both of them cast glances at me while their heads bobbed up and down. Then the bartender picked up a mobile phone. The call was brief. The waitress came back with my check, looking anxious to collect my money and get away from me. I sat for a while listening to the snippets of chatter around me, waiting for Allen Skye to show himself. I was sure he would when he heard that a stranger, especially a Yank, was in the pub asking questions about him.

As an hour passed, half-empty glasses piled up on some of the tables, the smoke thickened, and the evening news played on the television. By seven o'clock, when there was still no sign of Skye, I rose from my corner perch and inched across the room. I made my way through the crowd at the bar toward the door. Then someone who looked like he was a wide receiver in the NFL blocked my path.

Like thunder, his voice rumbled out of his six-foot-plus frame— "I'm Allen Skye. You were looking for me?"

"I'm Star O'Brien. And yes, I'm looking for you. Can we sit down?" I gestured to a couple of stools at the bar. He nodded and turned his blond head and blue eyes in that direction.

As we sat, the bartender came with two pints of Guinness and then disappeared as quickly as a flash of lightning.

Skye was young; he didn't seem any more than twenty. Had Raymond Nolan sent me on a wild goose chase? This guy looked like good old American apple pie and ice cream. Along with the blond hair and blue eyes, he had two dimples that were in full view because he kept smiling. Hard to imagine him as a drug dealer.

"So what can I do for you, Star?"

The dimples and grin persisted. I figured the cockiness was his primary personality trait.

"You can tell me about your friend Matthew Sumner. I'm investigating his death for his family. I'd like it if you could give me your thoughts on what type of person he was and who his other friends happened to be. Also, how often you two went boating around Clare Island."

I hoped Skye wouldn't realize that I knew nothing about their relationship other than what Raymond Nolan had told me.

"Oh yea, I heard about poor old Matt. Too bad."

"So, you did know each other?" I paused, waiting for him to fill in the space. But he wasn't going to let me get the upper hand. I realized that groveling or lying would be necessary to get him to give up what he knew. I've found that looking into families' secret lives sometimes requires extraordinary efforts.

"Oh yea, he wasn't a bad fella to have around once in a while. The girls liked him."

Boy would I love to wipe that smirk off his face. But I knew that wouldn't work. Using my softest voice, I whined instead.

"I'm not very good at this kind of thing. But Matthew's sister asked me to talk to people about his spiritual and emotional health just before he died. You seem like the kind of person who'd understand a lot about someone's psychology. I only have a few questions and then I'll get out of your life."

Boy, I made myself sick with this approach. But it worked because he shrugged by way of consent and scanned around the bar as if to gauge who was watching and listening to us. He must have decided the coast was clear.

"You want me to tell you about Matt for your investigation?" he asked while one of his eyebrows rose quizzically at me. The dimples were gone now. "And what do I get for this effort? What's the quid pro quo?" He downed his pint of Guinness, watching me all the while, then motioned to the bartender for another one.

I daintily moved my glass around and waited. I also marveled at the aggressiveness and fearlessness that youth brings with it. How could someone so beautiful be so ugly inside? I wouldn't want to meet him alone in an alley one night.

Clearly, this discussion would be like panning for gold. I'd get a lot of dirt and grit, and maybe only a nugget. And I might not recognize the nugget right away.

"I found his body," I told him, knowing full well it wasn't true. "I also know that he made some secret trips to Dublin recently."

"That's a lie," he replied quickly. "I was at the inquest. You and the entire population of Clare Island found the body. And I know that Matt visited Tranquility House, if that's what you mean by secret trips to Dublin. In fact, I recommended it to him." He crossed his arms over his chest. His secrets were obviously locked up tight, and I still hadn't found the right words to open the safe. But what he said confirmed that his link to Matthew was through drugs.

"Was he a client of yours?" I parried back. "Is that why you recommended Tranquility House?"

"I don't have clients, Miss O'Brien. I have a family of dependents. They depend on me for their bliss, their version of reality. Matt had his own sense of reality; I couldn't sell him mine."

"What was his interest in Tranquility House then?"

"He had many interests and problems. I recommended Tranquility as a possible solution to those problems." He yawned and surveyed the bar.

I'd lost him, at least for the moment. So, I decided on another bluff and more lies.

"Matthew was interested in the owner of a particular motor boat," I said. "Some of the residents on Clare Island say it was frequently anchored around the island's coves and inlets. His diary describes dates, times and places that he'd seen it. A log of the tides was plotted in conjunction with the information. Any ideas about why he'd do that?"

Skye's eyes bored into mine like a power drill into solid wood. "Whose boat? What's the registration number?"

Bingo! I had his attention.

"As you said earlier, what do I get in exchange for my information?"

Skye shrugged, studied my face, and seemed to consider what to do next.

"Okay, you've got a deal," he said. "But I want that diary."

This was getting out of hand. My inner conscience screamed at me to stop lying. But then why should I? I didn't owe Skye the truth. He was a drug dealer, and I had a client whose brother was dead, possibly because of this very man.

I took a deep breath and smiled at him.

"I don't have it. I turned it over to the police. But I remember what was in it, and I made copies of the pages with the schedule of comings and goings of the boat."

"I'll tell you what I know," he said, "but you'd better not be lying to me. I'll want copies of those pages. You can send them to this address." He reached into his pocket and handed me a business card. It had his name and address, the latter a post office box.

I turned the card over. On the back it read 'Skye Consulting: The Sky's the Limit.' Jeez, even crooks had business cards.

I stuck the card in my jacket pocket and waited for him to speak again.

"I run an enterprise. I sell people their version of happiness. It's a small business venture. My target audience are computer and technology experts." He stopped, tilted his head toward the bartender, who rushed over with another pint, before continuing. "They make good salaries and can afford my services. They consider themselves trendy." As he took another drink of his Guinness, the dimples reappeared.

My stomach turned over, and I wanted to run as far as I could from this piece of scum masquerading as a human being. But I couldn't. I didn't. My life was in danger, and I had to find out who murdered Matthew. I waited for him to continue.

"It's come to my attention that there's a larger operation in the area," he said finally. "Someone is dealing in a variety of drugs, and to a greater geographical area. Through my own contacts, I haven't been able to determine who's behind it." He paused to push the Guinness glasses between us aside in order to lean toward me. "And although my business is a conservative one, this bigger fish is cutting into my revenues and costing me opportunities. I want to protect my assets. Business has been good during the past few years. I've purposely kept my operation small. I mean why should I be greedy?" He smiled like a choir boy.

"So what was Matthew's connection to all this?" I asked.

"He was aware of my business. He threatened me. Said if he found me dealing to anyone, he'd kill me. He mentioned Clare

Island. He had it in his mind that I received my supplies by sea out there. I don't, but it made me curious."

So that was it—market share and revenues. Skye wanted to eliminate the competition. And it occurred to him that I might know who that was.

"Why did Matthew talk to you about Tranquility House then? He must have known about the facility through his work with Save the People."

"He did." Skye smiled and took another drink.

"So who did he want to send to Tranquility House?"

"I can't tell you that. It wouldn't be ethical, would it, if I revealed family secrets?"

He got to his feet and slapped twenty euros on the bar.

"I've told you all I'm going to. Now if you don't mind, I have a business to run. Don't forget those copies or you'll be hearing from me," he said, then swaggered out of the pub.

I LEFT A FEW MOMENTS LATER IN SEARCH OF SOME FRESH AIR. As I did, I glimpsed Sharon and Raymond standing on the corner of Linenhall Street. It might have been the cast of the green and yellow traffic lights, but I thought Sharon looked worse than when we'd met. Huddled inside a brown raincoat with her hands stuck in the pockets, she leaned her head toward Raymond, listening intently to whatever he was saying. The hand that he'd used to hammer his desk when we met now gripped Sharon's elbow. He stood above her, his face hovering within two inches of hers. His lips moved continuously. Sharon shook her head vigorously and tried to pull away, but he wouldn't let go. I pictured a bulldog with a bone in its grasp.

Determined to break this up, I strode to the corner calling out Sharon's name. Hearing my voice, they flinched as if an alarm bell had sounded in the middle of the night. Raymond dropped his hand. Sharon stepped back, turned on her heel, and scurried away before I could reach her. Raymond raised his fist at me and hurried off in the opposite direction.

At that moment, the ribs and sauce began dancing in my gut. Oh, I felt terrible. If I didn't put something neutral into my stomach soon, I'd have a whopping case of indigestion not just from having to swallow Skye's garbage but from the meal, too.

But first I had something more important to do.

I drove back to the cottage. As soon as I could, I dropped all my clothes in the laundry and got under a hot shower. The sooner I could wash off Skye's filth, the better off I would be.

Washed clean from head to toe, I toweled off and picked a container of hazelnut yogurt from the refrigerator. While the warmth of the fire in the living room dried my hair and warmed my soul, I replayed my discussion with that slime. I knew I'd have to make another circuit out to Clare Island to chase down his references to a bigger drug operation. From there I'd get back to Sharon and Raymond. Who could Matthew have been protecting? Either one of them, I guessed, since they'd all been so close.

What a night! First there were Allen Skye's revelations about Clare Island, and now this obvious confrontation between Matthew's fiancée and friend. I wondered what secrets they and Clare Island possessed concerning his death.

CHAPTER 16

When I awoke in the morning, something was wrong. Silence besieged my solitary cell of a bedroom. The usual droning airplane and whishing car tires were not there. Possessed, the cottage shuddered on its foundations. The wind moaned up and down the chimney. The front door shivered. Windows rattled, holding back the assault. Trees bent with the wind's forceful gusts. The rain beat down.

Would my spirit hold up to life's assaults the way this cottage did? Although, I'd lost my mother, the O'Brien's, and Dylan, their collective love had seen me through each storm. But sometimes I'm uneasy about the future. Would something finally break my spirit?

I hugged the bed and the hot-water bottle, from the night before, drew my feet toward it like a magnet. By six thirty, I knew that I wouldn't be getting any more sleep. Instead I got up and headed to the kitchen for breakfast. The wind had subsided and the rain misted. Toward the south, the sky was clear and bright. I'd stick with my plan to go to Clare Island later in the day. Meanwhile, I fell into my usual breakfast routine of brown bread, hazelnut yogurt, flax oil, and rhubarb.

As I'd suspected, the sun was out by the time I finished

eating. After throwing on my jogging pants, sweatshirt, and sneakers, I picked up the phone to make some calls. Peter's phone rang, but neither he nor his answering machine picked up. I'd hoped he could join me when I went to talk to Richard O'Malley. I wanted Peter's opinion about O'Malley and what I'd learned so far.

I called Bridget next. I brought her up to date on my visit to Tranquility House, and told her I planned to return to Clare Island that day. She thanked me and said she'd be away in Dublin for a few days.

"Will you be needing me?" she asked. Her voice sounded tired and soft over the phone.

"No," I assured her, and we said goodbye.

My fingers paused over the keypad, putting off the hardest calls for last. These were the ones to my friends and my team in the United States. Quickly I dialed; making the most difficult first.

"Hello," Joanne said. It took a moment for me to steady my voice when I heard her.

"Hi, it's Star."

"Star, oh my gosh!" she said. Then the questions came at me rapid fire—"Where have you been? When are you coming home? Have you sold that place? We miss you!"

Joanne owns a catering company in Ridgewood, and she's always rushing between appointments or running to check something in the oven.

"Well, I'm undecided about the cottage, and it may be a few more weeks before I'm home. The paperwork on this end is complicated." I paused to take a deep breath before continuing. "I'm calling to see how things are going and how Skipper is holding up."

"Skipper is fine. He'd been moping around, but then we got a new neighbor. You remember the Dutch Colonial on the corner of Katherine Street that was for sale? Well it sold, and they've already moved in. They have a female Pomeranian named Phoebe, so Skipper is in love. Since they met, he's parked himself at the top of the stairs, watching through the front door and waiting for her to walk by."

"Thanks Joanne. I'll really owe you for this. Do you think you can handle him for a while longer?"

"No problem girlfriend. You don't have to worry, we'll take good care of him.

"How is it over there?"

"We're roasted," she said. "I'm keeping cool by testing a new recipe for chocolate chip mint ice cream. It's delicious. Oh, and I've talked to the cleaning crew at your house a few times. They miss you too. But it's the Consulting Detective team that's getting dusty. Ellie and Philomena wonder if you're ever coming back. You'd better call them today."

"That's my next call when we hang up here," I told her. "I'll be in touch."

"Don't forget. We miss you. We love you and we want you home."

I waited for my tear-filled eyes to clear, then I dialed my home office.

"The Consulting Detective, Ellie Pizzolato speaking."

"Hey Ellie, it's Star."

"I'm so glad you called. It's getting a little crazy working in this tree house you call a home office without you. Why haven't you checked in recently?"

When Dylan and I remodeled the old colonial we bought, we installed separate home offices. Mine was on the top floor just below the tree tops. I'd designed it to have the feel of a tree house, with ceiling-to-floor glass windows and a deck along the back that overlooked a brook. In the summer when the trees bloomed, we lived in a jungle.

"Something came up over here that I'm investigating," I

said. "Listen, is Philomena there? I want her to do some research for me."

"She's here today. But you have to deal with me first." As usual, Ellie didn't waste time with the niceties—she was all business. "What do you want me to do with this email that you've been avoiding? Didn't we agree that you'd use a local internet café while you were away to handle it? But you haven't touched it in days. And we have a request for a new research project that you need to approve before I process the contracts with the potential client."

"I promise I will get into email and clear it out when I have a few minutes. I just don't trust the internet cafés; you know this stuff drives me crazy. I don't want anyone screen- scraping information." I played with the phone cord, feeling equally twisted about my security dilemma. "Tell me about the new contract."

"Your potential client is the twenty-year-old daughter of a famous model who died when the kid was five months old," Ellie said. "The daughter's recently come into full control of the trust fund her mother set up, and she wants to find her father. This story may end up in the press, and I want to make sure you're ready to handle it if that happens."

'Go ahead and take it, Ellie. I'll handle the press. It's more important that the kid finds her father. Now, can I speak with Phillie?"

"Not so fast, Star. Where will you be when the calls start coming in? I want to know where they can find you." Her tone underlined the word *you*.

"I promise. I'll handle it. Now put Phillie on."

"Hold, please...."

A few beats of silence followed, then a different voice came on the line.

"Hi Boss, Ellie says you have an assignment for me."

Philomena Spring—Phillie—is my part-time technical

guru, who spends the other part of her time blogging about women, technology, and innovation. She calls me boss although I've asked her a million times to call me Star. She usually points out that I'm not a star and keeps on calling me boss.

"Hi Phillie, yes, I need you to do some research. Anything you can find on a foundation called Save the People, its director Raymond Nolan, a woman named Sharon Dawson who is formerly a broker for Merrill Lynch but now a financial investment adviser, and a business called Sumner Family Farms. They grow mushrooms. Give me a call here when you find anything."

"Okay."

Click.

And just like Ellie, Phillie got right down to business.

My calls made, I showered, donned cropped pants, a pink t-shirt, and flats. With Allen Skye's threat fresh in my mind, I skipped my walk, feeling too edgy and nervous about what he might do. I packed my knapsack with a change of underwear, sneakers, my passport, wallet, and Matthew's notes on the tides around Clare Island. I'd stop in town and make copies to mail to Allen.

As I opened the back door to leave, the phone rang. It was Phillie again. She was phenomenally speedy at mining the data and tuning the computer keys.

"Nothing on Sharon Dawson. Press releases, speaking engagements, the same old, same old financial services statements. You know the drumming up business kind. Nada on the mushroom family as well."

"You mean Sumner Family Farms. Right?" Phillie tends to create nicknames for people and organizations.

"Yeah, the 'shroom people. Nothing in their financial statements that's out of the ordinary. But the other group, the Save the People. Their fundraising hasn't been what it was in the past. Looks like a downward spiral, if you know what I mean, boss."

"Thanks, Phillie. If you find anything else call me. Okay?"

"Yeah."

Click again.

THERE'S NOTHING LIKE A DECLINE IN SPONSORSHIP TO SPIKE pressure. No wonder Nolan was tense. It could drive him to do anything. I opened the back door and made my second attempt at leaving when the phone rang once again. It was Peter this time.

"I tried you earlier this morning," I said.

"Oh, what time?"

"It must have been about nine."

"I guess I was out walking," he replied. "Sorry I missed you."

"I'm on my way to Clare Island today."

"You are? What's your plan?"

"You sound surprised." I hesitated. Was I rushing our relationship? I hoped he didn't think I was coming to Clare Island only to see him.

"I'm planning on talking to Richard O'Malley again, and trying to make better sense of Matthew's notes and how they relate to the terrain out there."

"I'm not surprised, Star," Peter said. "Merely disappointed that I won't be here tonight or tomorrow. I'm going to Dublin. A rare handmade English grandfather clock dating from the 1600s has turned up. I've got to strike before anyone else snaps it up. I know someone who's been looking for one of these for a long time. I may make an extra commission on this if I can get my hands on it first."

"Well, have a great trip," I said plainly. In fact, I was disappointed, but I didn't want him to know that.

"Will you be staying at the Lighthouse Cottage?"

"No. Since I only expect to be there overnight, I'm staying at The Seabreeze. It's not far from the harbor and the hotel, so it'll be easy to get out to O'Malley at the Abbey early in the morning."

"Do you think O'Malley knows anything significant?"

"Well, he knows the island. And I have more information now than when we first met. Maybe with that and any suspicions he might have, I'll make some progress."

Peter's sigh carried perfectly clearly through the line. "I hoped you'd have told Bridget by now that this is a dead-end matter."

"But it isn't. I've definitely linked Matthew's activities before he died to a drug rehab program and a local small-time drug dealer named Allen Skye. When I figure out what on Clare Island interested Matthew so much, I think I'll be able to reconstruct what happened to him."

"Promise me you won't do anything or go anywhere unless you've discussed it with me first," he said. "After what happened in Dublin the other day, someone should know your whereabouts all the time."

"Aunt Georgina always knows how to reach me," I told him. I imagined what he'd say if he knew about the anonymous threat that I'd received.

"Listen, I'd like to have dinner with you again. I'll be back in Castlebar on Tuesday. Can I pick you up at eight?"

I smiled. "I'll look forward to it."

"Great. See you then. And, Star, be careful—rough seas are forecasted."

Remembering my comment about Aunt Georgina always knowing my whereabouts, I left a message on her home machine about my plans for the day. Placing the phone back in its cradle, I felt good about my decision to have dinner with

Peter again. I'd never dated a man with dark eyes and hair the color of ebony. Chuckling to myself, I wondered how many other women had fallen under his spell.

THE ROONAGH PIER WAS DESERTED. A FEW SMALL BOATS BOBBED up and down between the chop in the distance. I'd made a call to the harbor master earlier in the day to let him know that I'd received permission from the Sumner's to board their boat. He'd agreed to meet me at the quay that afternoon. Not long after I arrived, he drove into the parking area and gave me a wave as he leapt from his car.

"Hello! Are you Star O'Brien?" He covered the ground between us with the speed of a hare. "I don't have much time. I've got another appointment shortly in Louisburg. I understand you have some questions." He spoke as fast as he walked.

"This won't take too much of your time," I said. "The Sumner's have asked me to investigate their son's death."

"Oh right. Poor lad. What can I tell you?"

"I'm wondering about his use of the boat. Who might have been with him when he used it? Things like that."

"Aye, he did use it. Although I can't really tell you much. Take a look around." He raised his arm to indicate a wide sweep of the road leading to the quay. "This is a deserted area, miles away from the closest town. In fact I don't even man the place full time. It's a part-time thing for me. I own a boat of me own, and the stipend keeps me in petrol." Shaking his head, he bent to pick up some empty soda bottles before continuing. "The Sumner lad did take the boat out, and the few times I saw him it was at night. Once in a while, if I happened to be back here the next morning, I'd see that the boat hadn't returned yet. So he must have made overnight trips as well."

"Did he ever mention where he was going?"

"No, we didn't talk much. He kept to himself. As do most of the folks around here."

"How about passengers? Did you ever see anyone with him?"

"Oh yeah, a few times he was with a fine-looking lassie. I assumed she was his girlfriend. Jet black hair and petite."

I nodded. "Did you ever talk to her?"

"Lord no. The few times I said 'how are ye?' she turned away and ignored me. Very pretty, but had a kind of coldness if you know what I mean. Now that's all I can tell you. I have to get to town. Is there anything I can help you with regarding the boat?" He pointed over to the general dock area.

"No, I know my way around boats. I'll take a look and get back to you if I have further questions."

"Right then. Be careful, the water's getting choppier. There's a nasty storm heading in."

He vanished as quickly as he'd appeared. Then I noticed that he drove a Volkswagen Rabbit. *Could there be a correlation?* I wondered.

The Sumner's boat was an offshore forty-four-foot Island Packet sailboat called *Shroom*. Seeing the name, I chuckled and thought of Phillie. From the looks of the high-tech navigational equipment on the boat, the family business must be good. I took a quick look around top side before going into the interior. Several charts for the coastal waters and for Clare Island were clipped near the captain's chair. I used Bridget's key to turn the power on and check the fuel tanks. They were almost empty. I'd have to ask if she knew whether they'd been left full by her or her parents.

When I stepped into the narrow companionway, I pulled its hatch down behind me for privacy. Unlike the meticulously organized topside, the berth area hadn't seen housekeeping in a while. The bed was unmade, with rumpled sheets and a duvet cover half hanging on the floor. Blond and dark strands of hair

commingled on the pillows. One of Sharon's business cards was
stuck into the side of the mirror that hung on the back of a
closet door. Sharon and Matthew must have been the most
recent occupants, I decided. I became sure of this when I saw
the dirty salt-rimmed glasses in the kitchen galley. A glass-
topped table had scratch marks and residual white powder.
The results of making margaritas, or was it something more?
Looking closer, the white substance looked granular to me, like
sea salt. I wondered if the police had searched the boat. Probably not.

Just as I reached forward to touch the granules, I heard footsteps crossing the boards above me. I held my breath and
listened. Steady movement overhead. Perhaps it was the harbor
manager; maybe he'd forgotten to tell me something. I turned
to head up the companionway and open the hatch. He might
not even know I was down here.

When I got to the stairs, the hatch was open—although I'd
closed it. Cautiously I made my way up. Barely breathing, I
peered toward the sky and inched my head above the opening.
There was no one in sight. The boat rocked back and forth as I
steadied myself and looked for the harbor master's VW Rabbit,
but only my car occupied the parking lot. Clanging halyards
slapping against the masts of the boats in the yard clamored
from the increasingly gusting winds. *So it must have been the
wind that lifted the hatch to the companion way.*

At least that's what I told myself.

CHAPTER 17

The *Ocean Star* limped into Clare Island's harbor around eight o'clock. And just like this tired old ferry, I felt like a rag that'd been wrung out until there was nothing left. Captain O'Malley's lips, compressed into a thin white line, never uttered a word. Instead, his hands gripped the wheel like glue, guiding his bucking vessel through the whitecaps and gusting winds.

Hopeful that my land legs would continue to hold me; I walked off the quay and headed up the mountain toward the bed and breakfast. During my visit to the island before Matthew's death, I'd stopped in front of the Seabreeze Bed and Breakfast often to admire the view of the beach and harbor. Several times I'd spoken to the owner, Mary Moran, about living on an island year-round. I liked her stories about the joys of waking to the view of the sea that stretched out to the coast. I also liked the resiliency it required to cope with isolation during the winter, when forceful billowing winds often prohibited travel to and from the mainland. Mary and I had developed an instant camaraderie when we discovered that we both loved mysteries, especially Deborah Crombie's 'Kincaid and Jemma' series. We promised to keep in touch via email.

Further up the heights at the lighthouse, darkness

surrounded Peter's place. He must have made it off the island before the winds picked up. But that was neither here nor there at the moment—I couldn't think of anything but sleep and was happy to step over the threshold into Mary's cozy sitting room.

A blazing turf fire burned in the grate. Mary and her husband Tom were sprawled in matching recliners, watching a special on RTE, the Irish television network. Then we chatted for a few minutes about the ride across and the winds.

"The forecast calls for winds over a hundred and thirty-five kilometers tonight," Tom said as he lent forward and poked the turf sods.

I don't care what it does now that I'm on land, I thought.

"At least it will keep everyone inside," Mary said, "including the drug smugglers." Then she shook her head. "This island is getting like one of my mystery stories."

"Are you talking about Matthew Sumner's death?" I asked.

Both she and Tom nodded in agreement.

"I don't always sleep well," Mary continued, "and a few times I saw him late at night on the beach. Maybe I really have read too many mysteries, but I'd swear I saw him flicking a flashlight on and off."

"Did you tell the police about this?"

"The guards? No. They didn't talk to us. And what does it prove really?" Mary shrugged.

"Are you sure it was Matthew?"

"Oh yes. I'm certain. You couldn't miss that bleached blond head of hair. When he flashed the light, I saw him very clearly."

After showing me to my room, Mary tried to entice me with homemade vegetable soup. But my stomach was still on the *Ocean Star,* churning with each wave that slapped into the boat.

I crawled into bed, thankful for the hot-water bottle that had been placed near the footboard. The room's sterility soothed more than a sedative. The walls were white, a Sacred Heart picture their solitary adornment.

Sacred Heart pictures, with a list of family member names inscribed at their bases, are a common sight in Irish homes. It's a devotion to, and belief, in the Sacred Heart's protection of the home and family.

Mary's guest room contained a twin pine bed, night table, and painted wooden chair. The chair served a dual purpose as it held my clothing. There was nothing in here to clutter my thinking, either. I could leave all my worries, like unnecessary furniture, at the door. In the morning, feeling fresh and renewed, I was confident I'd find the answers to Matthew's death. And if I could find answers for that, perhaps I could find some in the search for my mother as well. In the meantime, I snuggled into the warmth of the bed and wrapped my arms around myself. I fell asleep listening to the symphony of leaves shimmying on bushes and the rise and fall of the wind.

I woke the next morning around six thirty. It would be at least another hour, I knew, before any other creature in the house stirred. The sound of the wind had evaporated, and I saw patches of blue sky intermingled with scattered white clouds. So the storm was over. I wished my life could be like the weather—one good storm once in a while to clear out the turmoil and worries, and then clear skies after that.

I wondered at the moment what I might do with the rest of my life. Would I look back one day and wish I'd chosen a different path? Up until now, the choices had been easy. I didn't regret anything or any of the time spent with Dylan. But he was gone, and I wasn't sure that the past could be my anchor in the future. Dylan, my family, my background, and my past were all gone. Where was *my* Sacred Heart? Would finding my mother change any of that? Or would it all end in rejection? Should I spend my time creating a past or a future? And how linked were the two, really?

With no immediate answers coming to mind, I got up and

headed for the shower. I remained under the warm water long enough to wash away my questions.

WHEN I STEPPED OUTSIDE, I WAS GLAD TO SEE THAT THE SUN controlled the day. I greedily took deep breaths, inhaling the fresh ocean air. I stopped at the shop near the quay and stocked up on biscuits, fruit, and water for my day's meandering.

"I didn't think you'd be back here again," Mrs. Leonard said as she bagged up the items.

"I'm looking for Richard O'Malley. Have you seen him this morning?"

"Richard? Well, yes, he always on the island." She stopped, looked around the shop, and continued, "Of course, he seems to turn up everywhere. I wonder he can even get any work done with the time he spends walking around the mountain."

I noted that the scrape on her hand had healed but there was a pair of crutches behind the counter. "Are those yours?"

"Oh, those! I scraped up one of my knees again." She handed over my change along with the bag. "I'm getting too old for loading and unloading supplies. And, you'll probably find Richard out at the Abbey ruins."

The walk to the ruins took me past Grace O'Malley's castle, which sits low to the ground. It was an oblong-shaped structure with turret-type rooms projecting over the water on the eastern sides. The remnants of a stone passageway and a stairway, rising through three levels, pieced together just enough to form a holographic shadow of its former life.

I mused about Grace O'Malley, part myth and part reality. She survived until she was seventy almost four hundred years ago and still hasn't been forgotten. Had *she* ever worried about her past? What kind of mother did she have that inspired her to shave her head and become a mercenary sea captain like the male members of her clan? Did her body repose beneath the now roofless walls of the Abbey on Clare Island? I also couldn't help wondering why Matthew didn't have any paintings of the castle in his studio. He certainly had the opportunity to do some while working on the island.

I found Richard inside the Abbey's chancel. He wore gloves as he toiled on a slab of stone with his brushes.

"Hello," I said as I stooped down to fit myself into his workspace. "I hope I haven't come at a bad time."

"This is tricky work. Hold on a minute." He bent his head and body closer to the stone that he toiled over.

"I can come back," I suggested.

"No, just a minute...." He did a little more, then straightened his body up and beckoned me to come closer. "I'll show you a bit of history."

It was a wall mural. I could make out a rearing stallion and a wild boar. The name *O'Maille* appeared in large letters at the bottom of the slab.

"Beautiful, isn't it?"

"It is, yes."

He stared at it for a few moments, grinning. Then he turned and said, "So what can I do for you, Miss O'Brien? I take it you're still trying to figure out the facts behind Matthew's death?"

"I am, and I have some more questions for you. I'm afraid I need an hour of your time and attention."

O'Malley glanced at his watch. "This work here is obsessive, and when my artistic muse is active I need to follow her lead lest she decide to abandon me." He chuckled, checking the time again. "So why don't we have lunch at the Bay View Hotel? I'll meet you there in about two hours."

I nodded. "Okay."

With that settled, he didn't lose any time turning back to his stone slab.

WITH AN ABUNDANCE OF TIME ON MY HANDS, I HEADED FOR THE shoreline. I glimpsed other small dots of land sprouting up in the bay. In addition to the fishing boats, jet skis rumbled up and down.

I removed Matthew's notes from my knapsack and reviewed them. They listed a series of dates in July right up to a week before his death. Next to each date he had written times, most at night, and had drawn a picture of the island with three X's marked along the west side, well away from the quay.

Using a tourist map of the island from my earlier visit, I hiked to where Matthew had drawn one of the X's on his crude map. This particular X was along the shoreline closest to the Abbey. The terrain was grassy, and it was easy to walk across fields toward the water's edge. Then it got a little tougher as I picked my way over rocks and stones.

What did the X's indicate? I wondered. Did they mark places that Matthew had scrutinized? Or were they meeting or hiding places? This first one couldn't be a hiding place. The location was too open and accessible. But as in Poe's *The Purloined Letter*, isn't the best place to hide something out in the open? A boat captained by someone who knew the area wouldn't have any problems navigating the rocks that lurked beneath the blue water. And this side of the island was less inhabited than the quay. Even if someone saw a strange boat—or anything else for that matter—they might not have said anything. The Irish believe that a good neighbor is someone who minds his or her own business, after all.

Wanting to see if I could pinpoint the area marked by the other two Xs, I turned north. My intention was to climb one of the paths that winds further up the western side of the island, and ultimately to the heights of Knockmore Mountain. It didn't take long to break a sweat. I stopped to drink water and nibble on a biscuit. The wind was still strong, and the vertical climb was so steep that I had to grab bits of tuft sticking out of the ground to continue. Then the path petered out and turned into bog.

I couldn't continue without proper hiking boots. The ground was slippery, the cliff edge closer than I wanted it to be. If I lost traction and fell, I'd end up like Matthew. I couldn't help wondering if perhaps his death was accidental after all. Even a goat would have to be careful on this terrain. What was he even doing up here? Maybe he fell from the cliffs and his body drifted into the quay.... But if that were so, it didn't explain his trip to Dublin or conversations with Allen Skye. Nor did it explain the cocaine he'd had in his pocket.

Maybe O'Malley can answer some of these questions, I thought as I turned to find my way back down. Then, when I twisted my torso, my left foot got stuck in a rutted piece of the path and didn't follow. After I lost control of my body and ended up lying on my back with my foot twisted beneath me, I cursed my preoccupation with turning ideas over in my mind. Staring at the sky, I slowly raised myself to a sitting position and felt my ankle and foot. Relieved that it wasn't broken (but would probably hurt like hell for a day or two), I heaved myself back into a standing position.

"*Madre mio!*" gasped a voice a few feet away from me. "You scared me to death! Where did you come from?"

Recognizing Lucia, I said, "Hi, my name is Star O'Brien. I'm a friend of Matthew's sister Bridget. Do you think you can give me a hand down the mountain?"

"I will, yes," she replied, tucking her stocking cap into her back pocket.

Although I wouldn't recommend almost falling off the side of a cliff for any reason, I realized that my situation created the perfect opportunity to talk to the teenager about her relationship with Matthew. Limping down to where she stood, I handed her my knapsack. Then I proceeded to gently put one foot in front of the other as I led the way back down the path.

"So, you are a friend of Matthew's sister?" Lucia asked, catching up with me to walk abreast. Her hiking boots went effortlessly over the rugged path as if they were on automatic pilot. An artist's sketch book and pencil peeked out of the over-sized front pockets in her denim overalls. Compared to when I'd seen her after Matthew's body was found, Lucia appeared quite composed.

"Yes," I said. "If you don't mind, I'd like to hear more about his life on the island. I happened to be here the day his body was found, and I remember that you knew about his work at the Abbey."

A brilliant smile illuminated her blue eyes and porcelain skin. "Yes, Matthew taught me about his work as an art histori-an!" she gushed. "Sometimes when my mother allowed me free time from my studies, I would visit him at the Abbey. He showed me how to draw the Celtic knots and loops he created for the project."

"He must have thought you're talented. Do you paint?"

Her eyes widened. "Oh yes, I love to paint. Matthew believed I might be eligible for a scholarship at the University in Dublin." She turned her gaze toward the fishing boats bobbing in the water before continuing, "He promised to get me the application forms and guide me through filling them out and preparing my project for presentation. He was wonderful."

My heart went out to her. It can't be easy as a teenager living on a remote island in a strange country. It was obvious that his interest in her painting talents had fostered her crush on him, although Lucia's fragile beauty guaranteed that she'd be noticed no matter where she went.

"Did Matthew seem different to you lately?" I asked.

She considered her answer carefully. "Not different, but

quieter. And he sometimes cancelled our lessons because he said he wanted to go for a walk around the island. I thought maybe he'd changed his mind about my abilities as an artist."

Oh, the emotional rollercoaster ride of the teenage years, I thought. Boy, did I remember a crush I'd had on Timmy Lawson, the college-age boy who'd lived across the street from the O'Brien's. How many times did I imagine that he was in love with me? All the while he had a steady stream of college-age girlfriends.

"Do you really think he changed his mind about helping you?" I went on, trying a different approach. "From what I've learned about him, he seems like someone who kept his word. Maybe he was worried about something or someone else? Did he ever have any visitors?"

"That stupid girlfriend of his was here, and they had an argument and...." She halted the flow of words, plunking her hand over her mouth.

"And what, Lucia?"

"Whatever," she shrugged and dropped my knapsack on the ground next to me. "I have to get back." Then she waved her hand toward the water. "My mother will be angry when my father tells her I spoke with a stranger."

In the next instant she was gone, leaving me to wonder what it was she didn't want to tell me.

I picked up the knapsack and limped slowly down the mountain toward the hotel, and didn't stop until I got there.

CHAPTER 18

Everyone I'd spoken with avoided directly answering questions about Matthew. Raymond Nolan desired to defend his foundation. Sharon Dawson chose to detach herself from Matthew altogether. (*Was it because of her highly visible role as an investment advisor? I couldn't help wondering.*) And Richard O'Malley's career and sustenance banked on excavating and preserving historical sites and artifacts. How far would he go to ensure that his project continued? Would he withhold information? If so, how much? These were all questions I hoped to tackle during our lunch.

The Bay View hotel and pub, one of only two places for nourishment on the island, sits on a rise of land facing the harbor, the castle, and the sea. When Richard arrived, he placed a worn green army knapsack on the floor next to our table.

"Can't be too careful," he said as he eased himself into his chair. "Tools of my trade, you know. Have you ordered yet?"

"No," I replied. "I waited for you. I haven't seen a waitress since I sat down."

"Well, we'll fix that immediately. Mary!" he boomed. "Mary,

what kind of an establishment are you running here?! You've got customers!"

The attractive, tall brunette who materialized flashed a grin in my direction. "Richard O'Malley, if I'd known you were coming, I'd have rolled out the royal carpet. Richard's a descendant of the Kingly O'Malley's and as such we have to treat him like the nobility that he is." She winked at me as she leaned in over the table, prepared to take our order.

"That and a euro will get you a pot of tea," he told her. "Listen here, woman, bring a couple of Guinness and a menu while you're at it."

"No beer for me," I said, "but I'd love a diet Coke."

Richard looked surprised. "What no Guinness? Ah well, make it one then Mary."

Within a few minutes, the Guinness and menus appeared. We agreed on a basket of mixed toasted sandwiches consisting of cheese, chicken, and ham, as well as a basket of brown bread and homemade vegetable soup for me.

While we waited, I passed a copy of Matthew's notes to O'Malley.

"What about the dates?" I asked. "They're all in July, right up to the week before he died."

"Well, I'd need to check my accounting ledger to be sure, but I'm willing to bet that Matthew worked on the island on all these days. And we can check the marine forecasts and verify high and low tide times. I'm sure that's what these numbers imply."

"Couldn't they also indicate events such as the coming and going of a boat?"

Richard nodded. "Aye. Naturally enough, high and low tides would correlate to how far into the island's surrounding waters and close to shore a boat could come. If only I knew more about what he was involved in. I'm sorry he had the impression that he couldn't confide in me." I noticed that his voice trembled for one swift second there. "What about Nolan? Has he been able to help?"

"Nolan is about as helpful as a stone," I told him. "He believes Matthew was a drug addict and got caught up in a nasty dealing situation. The only insightful information he shared was to suggest that I speak to one of your more entrepreneurial citizens—Allen Skye."

I watched Richard closely to gauge his reaction to the name.

"How can Nolan be so pigheaded!" he erupted. "Matthew didn't have a drug habit! His work was his addiction. He lived and breathed two things—his art and his fiancée, Sharon."

"Okay, so what about Matthew's relationship with Sharon? I bumped into Lucia this morning, and her perception of their relationship differs from yours." I described my encounter with her on the mountain in detail.

"Ah, teenagers," he replied. "What could she know about the intricacies of an adult relationship? She does—I mean she *did*—have a crush on Matthew. That much was clear when she hung around the Abbey waiting for him. And no doubt she's talented. Matthew recognized that and encouraged her artistic abilities, but nothing more. I wouldn't set much store in what she says if I were you."

"Okay, what about Nolan's reticence to talk about Matthew? What do you think is behind that? And what can you tell me about Allen Skye? He and I had an interesting conversation which confirms what you're saying. He claims that there was a dependency problem in Matthew's family, but that it wasn't Matthew himself."

"I'm not a man that deals in gossip. I have no time for it. But for what it's worth, I hear that Save the People may have financial difficulties. Their success rate is trending downward, and some wealthy sponsors are making donations elsewhere. Maybe that's why Nolan is so closemouthed."

"That may explain why he always looks like someone is holding a shotgun to his head," I said.

"Well, whatever his problem is, you be careful. Mysterious accidents happen to people in Ireland on lonely roads where there are no witnesses. Look what happened to Matthew on this sparse, small island."

His words sent a chill up and down my spine. My heart beat rapidly in my chest as I recalled the anonymous note that I'd received.

"Do you think I'm in danger?" I asked, forcing my eyes not to waver as I watched his. I took a deep breath and waited for his reaction.

"Yes, you are in danger. Aren't you after telling me you've been talking to Allen Skye? He's been seen in a fishing boat recently in the harbor. Arrah! But don't you worry, we're watching him. He won't be bringing any of his dirt to Clare Island."

Richard seemed sincere, and I liked him. He said the islanders watched Allen Skye—but where were they when Matthew was wandering around? Where were they when he ended up dead on their beach with a gash in his head?

"Skye indicated that there's a bigger operation than his on the island," I said.

"I can assure you we haven't seen anything out of the ordinary," he replied, "But if that's really the case, then we need to be more vigilant, don't we? And get the guards involved if we learn anything."

He gulped down the remainder of his Guinness and waved his hand to Mary. She brought him another and promised to hurry up our food order from the kitchen.

We spent the remainder of lunch talking about Ireland. I found myself telling him about Dylan, my adoptive parents, and my search for my birth mother. Talking to him was easy. His warm brown eyes reflected his interest in my story.

He snorted when I poured out my disappointment that Dylan may have been friends with Allen Skye.

"Not likely," he said. "Skye keeps to himself. He has to in his line of business. Don't even let yourself go there. And Nolan's just trying to keep you off balance and out of his affairs."

Richard then told me his wife had died early in their marriage, and he never had the heart to fall in love again. Instead, he poured himself into his books and research. His last words to me that afternoon—*Life goes on, Star. Pick a place and create your own roots.* —echoed in my heart throughout the ferry ride and the drive back to Castlebar. I've always believed that by taking things one step at a time, eventually I'd create a path. Was I walking down my birth mother's path? And if I remained here or went back to the States, was I just living in the shadow of the years Dylan and I spent together?

BEFORE I KNEW IT, CASTLEBAR SPRANG UP BEFORE ME, AND I filed away my musings for future consideration. Suddenly thirsty, I headed toward the Davitt. Upon entering the restaurant, my pace quickened when I spotted Aunt Georgina. She held court in one of the corner booths, speaking to an older man. Just as I reached them, he said goodbye and walked off.

"Star, how are you?" Georgina said cheerfully. "Come have some tea. Any more nasty messages? Where have you been? Who have you seen? Did you go to Clare Island?"

I waited for the rapid machine gun fire of questions to subside before I began answering. "Yes, I've been out there, and I met with Richard O'Malley."

The waitress came to our booth, and I ordered a chicken salad sandwich with a glass of milk. My stomach growled, calling for food.

"You know I was just talking to Bernie Smith," she went on.

"He's the gentleman that was here when you came in. He's a solicitor in town. He told me the guards haven't found anything new since the inquest. It's pretty much regarded as an accidental death."

I shook my head. "I feel like I know Matthew now. His work, his love for Sharon, his volunteer work at Save the People, his paintings—all indicate his compassion and love for life. He was *involved* in living. There's no apparent reason for his so-called drug use."

"Star, you don't get motivated to use drugs. You get hooked. Maybe something happened when he was away at school. Maybe he experimented to see how drugs influenced his talent."

"Why is everyone so eager to condemn him?" I asked her. "Why not give him an opportunity to tell us his story? That's all I want to do—give voice to his words."

"I understand your sense of moral righteousness, Star. And God knows I got you involved in this. I blame myself for that. But you've been threatened. That changes everything as far as I'm concerned."

"That doesn't mean I can just walk away. Don't you see that it makes it even more critical to find out what happened? Not only for Matthew, but for me. I can't let this be." I rose and left money for the waitress on the table. "See you later."

I kissed her briefly on the cheek and headed to French Hill. I was tired and wanted to take a nap, but I reached for the phone instead and dialed Sharon's number. Her answering machine picked up.

"Sharon, this is Star O'Brien," I said. "I have some things I'd like to discuss with you. Please call me when you get this message. Perhaps we can meet somewhere in town this evening."

Then, I fell into bed and a dead sleep.

CHAPTER 19

The beeping of the phone broke my sleep. I reached for the alarm clock—just a few minutes after nine thirty in the evening.

"Call me, Boss," Phillie's message said. "It's important." She also mentioned that she was on her way to a dinner hosted by Research in Motion honoring Women in Technology. So I'd have to call her tomorrow.

Sharon, on the other hand, hadn't responded to the message I'd left.

As I drove toward the Brownsville Flats, I considered about what I'd say to her. It was time to apply a bit more pressure in order to find out more about her relationship with both Matthew and Raymond. Some of the questions I planned to ask were about the argument I'd witnessed between her and Nolan when I exited the Wagon Wheel pub. I wanted to know the last time she'd sailed with Matthew on the *Shroom*, and had it just been the two of them or did they have company? And if they did have company, who was it? I also intended to bring up Lucia and her relationship with Matthew, even though Sharon probably wouldn't like that. Perhaps in an emotional moment of anger she would finally divulge what she knew about Matthew's activities, and why she'd grown frigid on him even though they hadn't broken their engagement.

When I turned onto her street, I saw a crowd gathered in front of her place. I wondered if it was one of the many set-dancing events that Irish towns and villages hold during the summer. Maybe that's why she hadn't called. Then I saw the flashing lights—an ambulance, and a blue-and-white van displaying the word, "Garda."

Reversing the car, I drove several blocks away before parking. Sticking my shaking hands in my pockets, I wandered back to Sharon's street and joined the throng, who congregated on the sidewalk and spoke in hushed tones.

"What's going on?" I asked one of the women standing near me.

She bowed her head toward Sharon's place. "The lady who lives in that house...someone said she was strangled."

I held my breath and prayed for a miracle. "Is she dead?" I asked.

"Yes, poor girleen, strangled with a pair of tights. Lord, have mercy on us. Where is this country heading?"

Several women blessed themselves and nodded in agreement.

"How did it happen? Was it a burglary?"

This was a logical assumption, I thought, considering the priceless paintings hanging in Sharon's home. I wanted to believe it had nothing to do with me and my investigation.

"One of my lads had a key, you see," said someone else. She looked to be about forty. "He used to do odd jobs for her. Mowing the lawn and such. When she's in Dublin, he'd bring in her mail and newspapers. She didn't like anyone knowing when the place was empty. Well, my Tommy sees the newspaper tossed in the driveway and doesn't he decide to take it in. And there she is, stretched out in the living room, dead. Tommy came straight over home and we called the guards. He and his father are talking to them now." She halted, bursting into tears. "Just imagine that my boy could have been killed."

The other women formed a circle around her.

"Did you see anyone?" I asked, rapidly searching the crowd for familiar faces. Was the killer still here, I wondered, gloating over his or her handiwork? And was he or she waiting for the opportunity to do the same thing to me that had been done to Sharon and Matthew?

"No, oh no," the woman told me between sobs. "My son nearly died with fright. He took flight out of there like the devil was on his heels."

Everyone blessed themselves again.

"She was such a pretty thing," another woman said. "Who could have committed such a wicked deed?"

They all shook their heads in amazement.

"That's what beauty and wealth get you—" someone else chimed in "—trouble. Trouble always follows the pretty ones. You know her boyfriend died recently—from drugs! Maybe she was involved in that? Just because she had a good job doesn't mean she didn't associate with the wrong kind of people."

Several police appeared along the sidewalk, requesting everyone to return to their homes. I immediately turned away, as I didn't want them to spot me in front of Sharon's home. I expected I'd hear from them soon enough anyway.

My voice, after all, was on her answering machine.

~

MY EFFORTS TO FIGURE OUT WHAT HAPPENED TO MATTHEW HAD stirred up someone. That much was very clear now. And that someone was most likely the same person who choked out Sharon's life. And as I trudged in the direction of The Golden Thread, I ached with the knowledge that I might be at least partially responsible for her death.

The Golden Thread was closed, and it struck me that I should have realized that. There was so much I should have realized. I was like a sleepwalker, acting my part in a nightmare from which I couldn't awake. I needed to talk to someone, to feel the kindness and warmth of a human hand. So I continued toward the Davitt, hoping that Aunt Georgina would be there.

When I finally reached it, my feet were dragging as if blocks of cement weighted them down. Aunt Georgina sat in the same corner booth from three hours earlier. So much had changed in that time, I thought miserably. At least her face seemed like a beacon shining down from heaven onto hell.

"I tried to reach you at the house," she said. "I hoped you'd come here. Have you heard about Sharon?"

"I just came from her neighborhood," I told her. Then I slumped down into the seat across from her, wishing its sturdiness could shore up the vulnerability that now clung to my aching bones like an anchor.

A waitress appeared, placing a cup of tea in front of me.

Aunt Georgina reached over and tugged my hands. "What happened, Star?"

"She's dead. Whatever happened, she's dead. So it's over."

But even as I said this, I knew deep down that it wasn't over for me until I'd succeeded or failed at finding who had destroyed both Matthew *and* Sharon's life. I'd done what the police had done to Matthew. I'd judged Sharon guilty and I was wrong. Sharon's blood was on my soul, and I wouldn't rest until I'd found her killer.

Aunt Georgina's forehead wrinkled, and her eyes widened with concern. Then her hands gripped mine. "This stops here, Star," she said. "You have to go to the guards and tell them about the threatening letter and the car incident in Dublin."

"I'm sure that I'll have an opportunity to speak with them soon," I told her. "And I won't have to initiate the contact."

"Oh, why not?"

"I left a message on Sharon's answering machine about wanting to meet tonight. Once they hear that and remember that I was on Clare Island when Matthew was found, I'm sure they'll be very interested in me."

Chills worked their way down my spine. Is this how Sharon felt just before she died? I wondered. Who strangled her? Why didn't I get there earlier? I might have prevented her death. This once I might have had the power to save others from grief.

"Okay, but why wait?" Aunt Georgina demanded, raising her voice as she gripped the edge of the table. "You tell the guards what you know and that you're working for Bridget. Then you call her and tell her you're out of it. Star, this is a garda matter now. Bridget will understand. My God, girl, she won't want you involved after this!"

Sharon's face appeared in my mind, and I sensed her fear. She was alone, cold and terrified. Then the image disappeared, and I shivered, even colder, numb to my own fears.

"No, I won't do that!" I shot back, barely able to recognize my own angry voice.

"Why not?"

"I'm not giving up, Aunt Georgina. I'm going to find whomever did this. And I'm not really doing it for Bridget anymore. Now I'm doing it for myself, Matthew, and Sharon."

A surge of energy moved upward from the base of my spine, like a wildfire spreading through brush. Its warmth left no room for aches and chills.

I rose, threw some money on the table, and gathered up my belongings.

"I've got to do this," I said, "So don't try to stop me." Then I touched Aunt Georgina's shoulder and could sense her fear. She didn't say anything back, however.

I turned and headed out into the night.

CHAPTER 20

A black sedan obstructed the narrow lane like a roadblock, but I was resolved to face whatever lay ahead. I straightened my shoulders, carried my head high, nodded to the two men who were waiting at my gate, and strode toward them.

"Where's the convention, fellows?" I asked, opening said gate and heading to the kitchen door. The two men followed in my footsteps like chicks learning to walk after their mother.

Neither one smiled. Dressed conservatively—gray suits, periwinkle blue shirts, matching ties—they appeared to be in their late thirties, maybe early forties. The Hardy Boys, Irish edition, all grown up. The taller one was about six foot, had blue eyes, blond wavy hair cut short, and a nasty-looking scar gouged over his left eye. The shorter one was bald and carried a round stomach that looked like he'd swallowed a basketball. They carried their gray suits and hushed tones like two undertakers arriving to retrieve a body.

"Are you Star O'Brien?" the taller one asked.

I nodded. "That's me."

"We're detectives from the garda," he continued, flashing a badge in my face. "There's been an accident in town, and we believe you can help us. We'd like to ask you some questions."

I tilted my head as if completely confused.

"Accident? I haven't been involved in any accident. And how do I know you're really detectives?"

"If it makes you feel better, you can call the garda station. But I assure you that we are."

"Okay, come on in. But I still can't think of what this may be about."

I've never been good with lies. Probably because I hate when I'm on the receiving end of them. But I didn't get the sense at this point that they realized this.

They passed through the kitchen close on my heels, like two Irish bloodhounds. Then I directed them into the living room, where they sat down on the love seat facing the fireplace. Their broad shoulders tapped each other as they tried to look authoritative in such a tiny piece of furniture.

Then someone rapped on the kitchen door—the *bang, bang, bang* reverberated through the cottage. This really was turning into a convention.

"Excuse me for a moment," I said, striding off. I wasn't expecting anyone, although, at that moment I would have been happy to see my guardian angel.

Lorcan's face peered at me through the small glass panes set into the oak door's top half.

My God, I thought to myself, *I'm looking for a guardian angel, not a man who makes my blood boil and my palms sweat whenever I'm near him.*

"What do you want?" I asked, opening the door no more than a few inches. Next thing I knew, Lorcan's foot wedged itself through the open space, and he strode through the kitchen into the living room. I had to run to catch up with him.

"Tom, Jim," he said to my visitors. "I was on my way home and saw your car outside. It's not often I see you guys in my part of the county. You know my mam and I live close by, and she'll be worried if she sees detectives around the place! So what's going on?" Lorcan then proceeded to settle himself into one of the two wing chairs.

Meanwhile, I was angrily thinking that this was my house, and how dare he barge in like he owns the place. And he wasn't usually this gregarious. *What is he up to?!*

The tall man flashed a friendly smile. "Lorcan! How are ya doin yourself? And how is your mam? We haven't seen you at any of the football matches lately!"

"Gentlemen, it's late," I said, interrupting this delightful little reunion. "You mentioned an accident."

Lorcan looked at me in surprise. "Accident? What accident? Are you okay?"

His smile could melt an iceberg, and I almost dissolved in its warmth.

I managed a frown. "I'm fine," I told him, "but these detectives seem to think I can help them with something. Something I'm hoping they'll explain shortly. Maybe they'll even introduce themselves...."

I dropped into a chair and leaned back, congratulating myself having brought the conversation back on track. I glanced at Lorcan again. He smiled. *My God, the man is relentlessly happy.* Then I turned and looked expectantly at the two policemen.

"I'm Thomas O'Shea," said the taller one, "and this is my partner, James Keenan. As you've already gathered, we're detectives with the Castlebar Garda Unit." He nodded toward my other unexpected guest. "Lorcan knows us well. He's been a great help to the unit on many occasions, as well as a great opponent on the football field." Then O'Shea's grin disappeared. "But as I said before, we have to ask you some questions."

I glanced at my watch and frowned as if I had an appointment to keep. Inside I quivered like a bowl of jelly.

"Go ahead," I said, "I'm all ears."

"Do you know a woman named Sharon Dawson?"

As Tom spoke, Jim extracted a notepad out of his jacket pocket and prepared to write down my answers.

"Yes, I've met Sharon. What's the problem? Has something happened to her?"

My stomach cringed with this whopping example of feigned ignorance. In that instant, I anticipated that I might have to make an emergency dash to the bathroom.

"Aye, there's been an accident. A serious one I'm afraid. We're talking to everyone who knew her." Tom moved his body forward and perched on the edge of the sofa cushion. "Have you seen or spoken with her today, or in the last few days?"

My stomach muscles relaxed as the air fled my lungs. Okay, so it appeared that these two didn't know I'd been to her house to ask questions about Matthew. All they knew was that I'd left a message with my name and number. Now that I knew that, I decided to limit their knowledge for a little while. At least until I figured out what happened to her.

"I had dinner with Sharon last night," Lorcan said in a voice so low that I barely heard it. He was peering over his glasses at O'Shea.

My head swiveled toward him faster than a dog picks up a bone. *He and Sharon?* Now my stomach was burning with anger. How many women was he involved with? Wasn't it only a few days ago that I'd seen him having dinner with the one he'd introduced as his cousin?

Jim stopped taking notes and studied Lorcan.

"Did she mention any appointments or anyone that she planned to see today?" Tom asked him. Then Lorcan glanced over at me.

"No," he replied. "In fact, she said she'd had a busy few weeks with some high-powered clients. She mentioned staying at home, doing the crossword puzzle in the *Sunday Irish Times*, maybe calling some friends. You know the kind of thing. A lazy weekend."

O'Shea hesitated, staring at the floor before he continued.

"And what was your relationship to Sharon?"

Lorcan glanced over his glasses at me. I couldn't wait to hear his answer.

"It was a business relationship," he said finally. "Sharon handles estate planning matters for me and my mother."

Lorcan is the heir to a fortune through ownership of real estate, several large businesses, and numerous patents for his inventions. And although I didn't know any of the small details, it seemed logical that a broker handled his investments and financial planning. I guess it made sense to O'Shea as well, because he nodded his agreement and redirected his attention to me.

"And your relationship with Sharon? You said you met with her this evening. What about?"

The gloves were off. The casual tone he'd used with Lorcan was replaced with firmness and efficiency. Was he bluffing me? What more could they know other than the fact that I'd left a message on her answering machine?

I decided to gamble.

"I didn't meet with Sharon today," I replied. "I haven't even spoken with her recently."

This made Kennan look up from his notebook.

"How can that be?" O'Shea went on, barking his words like a machine gun's rapid fire. "You left a phone message on her answering machine. You met her this evening."

Lorcan interrupted, "Star, didn't you tell me that you planned to call Sharon for an appointment to help you with Dylan's estate here in Ireland?"

He smiled again. I felt my facial muscles begin to respond before I caught myself. I couldn't afford to smile at him right now.

"Oh, that. Yes, I did call. But she wasn't home, so I left a message," I looked directly into O'Shea's eyes. "That must be the message you're referring to, Detective. She never called me back."

"When did you last speak to Sharon directly?" he asked. He clearly wasn't giving up.

"I recall chatting with her in the last few weeks," was all I said. I wasn't volunteering anything that they didn't already know.

"Weren't you on Clare Island when Matthew Sumner's body was discovered?"

"Yes, I was one of a crowd of at least fifty people who happened to be there."

Lorcan cleared his throat and said, "Tom, what's happened? This all sounds very ominous."

O'Shea got up. Now he stood directly in front of me, with his back to Lorcan.

"Sharon Dawson is dead."

His eyes drilled directly into mine.

Fear twisted like a knife in my stomach. I knew he wanted to gauge my reaction—my words, movements, breathing. I steeled my face to remain calm and composed. Then Lorcan got up, closing the distance between us, and stationed himself behind my chair. He placed his hand on my shoulder.

"No," I said, "she can't be." I gasped the words out struggling to get air into my lungs. How I wished those words were true. How I wished I could change the facts.

"What happened, exactly?" Lorcan asked, his voice as deep and calm as ever.

"She was found in her home several hours ago," O'Shea said. "And, your voice is on her answering machine. That fact and your presence on Clare Island when her fiancé's body was found is attention-getting, to say the least."

If the detective thought he'd be able to scare me into admit-

ting something, he was wrong. Instead, much to my surprise, I
began to cry. Everywhere I turned these days, people died. Was
my life an ordered creation of sorrow and death? Was there
anything in this chaos that I could build into a meaningful
purpose for my existence?

Lorcan squeezed my shoulder. "Tom, this is a coincidence,"
he said. "Star was in an accident herself several days ago." He
went on to explain about the car in Dublin. "She's exhausted
and upset. So why don't we arrange for her to call you tomorrow, when she's had a chance to rest? I'll drive her to your office
myself."

O'Shea nodded slowly as he regarded my tear-stained face.
Then he took a deep breath. "Okay. I trust your judgment,
Lorcan. I'll see you both in my office tomorrow. And by the way,
Ms. O'Brien, I also knew Dylan Hill well. I had tremendous
respect for him."

He didn't explain any more about their relationship than
that, and I was once again surprised by how much I didn't know
about Dylan. But at that moment, I didn't have the time or the
energy to ask questions.

O'Shea and his partner headed toward the kitchen, and
Lorcan escorted them out the door.

I SLUMPED FURTHER DOWN INTO MY CHAIR, REPEATING *I AM ALIVE,
I will survive* in my head.

I had to convince myself that there was a reason why I was
caught up in these people's lives. Maybe my sole purpose was to
help others. Maybe by helping others, I'd regain my own soul
along the way. But I hadn't helped Sharon, had I? She was dead,
and I wondered if it was the result of my questioning Raymond
Nolan and Richard O'Malley.

Lorcan walked back into the room. His step was so light that I didn't hear him until he stood directly in front of me.

"Are you okay? You've had a terrible evening."

I arose and offered him my hand and a half-hearted smile. "Thanks. I'm sorry you had to lie for me."

"Well, it was only a half-lie. I did have dinner with Sharon last night."

"Did she say anything? Give you any clue? Was she frightened?"

"Nothing tangible. I've dealt with her on a business basis for the last five years. She was nervous and fidgety. Not as sharp as she usually was when she discussed my portfolio. She asked if I knew you. Told me about your visit to see her. Wanted to know if I trusted you."

"She must have suspected Matthew's killer," I said. "All this talk about distancing herself from him was probably a lie. If only she'd talked to me, talked to anyone for that matter, maybe she'd be alive tonight."

"Listen Star, Georgina told me about the threatening note you received in the mail. Whoever sent it knows where you live. In light of what's happened tonight, I really want you to consider extricating yourself from this mess. I can use my relationship with O'Shea and Keenan to clear up any misconstrued ideas they might have about you."

He squeezed my hand. The smile was gone. Now his blue eyes looked intent and concerned. Feeling both comforted and vulnerable by this, my testiness and inner strength returned.

"Thanks, but no thanks," I said. "I don't need anyone's help. I intend to find whomever did this. I know I'm in danger, but I don't trust my life to anyone but myself. Now if you don't mind, I want to be alone."

For a minute, it crossed my mind that Lorcan actually looked hurt. But then, with my hand still in his, he nodded.

"You're right. It is your responsibility to take care of yourself. Just let me know if you need me."

"Lorcan McHale. Get out of here now."

I threw his hand down, marched to the door, and held it open.

"See you soon, Star," he said. Then he was gone—and his touch lingered long after he'd vanished from view.

I closed the kitchen door and locked it. Then, on my way to the bedroom, I rechecked the front door. The old-fashioned slide bolt was in place. I didn't bother with any bedtime rituals. After dropping my clothes on the floor, I crawled under the sheets. And I left all the lights on.

I lay there repeating, "I am alive, I will survive."

But I was lying to myself. There is no security in life. Especially in the dark of night, even with the lights on.

Still, I fell asleep whispering "I will survive."

CHAPTER 21

Considering the events of the previous night, I awoke feeling rested and more resolved than ever. There was a connection between Matthew and Sharon's murders, and I was going to find it. I'd slept the sleep of the dead—deep, dark, and dreamless. Maybe the "I will survive" mantra worked.

Light streamed through the windows, and from the fixtures I'd left on the night before. I walked into the kitchen. The message light on my answering machine was blinking. I pressed the PLAY button.

"Star," Peter's voice rumbled out at me, "I'm thinking about you, and it seems like it will be an eternity before I see you on Tuesday. Call me so that I can hear your voice and know you are well."

I called back immediately, but his message machine picked up. While I listened to the recorded voice, I wondered what we'd all do without answering machines and cellphones. Now we can reach out to anyone at any time...yet we never seem to connect. Instead, we leave a trail of messages behind us, hoping and believing that someone is listening. I'd left a message for Sharon. Had she gotten it? Was she planning on calling me as Lorcan's comments about her being able to trust me indicated?

Or had someone else stood in her house listening to my voice? Someone who couldn't afford to let me see Sharon that evening?

I hung up on Peter's machine without leaving a message. Forty minutes later, after I'd power walked faster than ever before, I sat at the kitchen table reviewing everything.

O'Malley implied that he wanted to help clear Matthew's name, but not if it cost him the Abbey restoration project's funding grant. Was this enough motivation to want to kill? I hadn't found any connection between O'Malley and Sharon other than his knowledge that she visited the island, and his affirmation that Matthew loved Sharon. Although O'Malley was aware of the rumors surrounding Allen Skye, neither man had indicated that they knew the other. But O'Malley's comment about the islanders' knowledge of Skye and being able to deal with him smacked of vigilantism. There was motive there to rid the project and the island of Matthew if he'd gotten involved with Skye.

I didn't think Allen Skye murdered Matthew. He was another brand of monster: an insidious, parasitical killer claiming souls through his drug trade. He was sneaky and wouldn't overtly eliminate his competition or threats. I sensed that he'd gotten perverse pleasure from Matthew coming to him for help. Skye would want to hold that card over Matthew, or use him to get at his own competition.

All paths led me to Raymond Nolan. He worked with Sumner. He knew Allen Skye. His foundation linked him to people with drug dependency. Because of his prior medical training and his work, he could probably gain access to drugs or to others who had access. His sister died of an overdose. He was in Dublin when I had my mysterious accident. He knew Sharon Dawson. So what had he been doing yesterday when Sharon was killed? For someone who'd devoted his life to fighting drugs, why couldn't he be more cooperative? I was sure

he knew more than he'd told me. He had to have his own suspicions—unless, of course, he was responsible for both murders.
Maybe Save the People was a front for the bigger operation that
Allen Skye alluded to in our conversation. Maybe in some
twisted and misguided way, Raymond used drug money to fund
it. O'Malley was sure that the foundation had money troubles.

I knew Raymond wouldn't like it, but I had to talk to him
again. I called Aunt Georgina.

"Star, how are you?" she asked immediately. I realized how
worried she was when her voice didn't carry its customary
snappy pace. She spoke slowly, emphasizing each word. I hated
to think that I might be causing her such pain. She'd been
wonderful to me, like a mother since I'd met her.

"I'm fine," I replied. "I'm sorry I didn't call last night, but I
was exhausted when the police decamped here. Surprisingly,
though, I slept well. So, you see there's nothing to worry about."

"But I do worry about you. Now, tell me what's going on.
Why don't you come to the shop? I've got appointments that I
can't cancel this morning, but I want to see you for myself."

"I may be able to stop by later in the day," I told her, "but
right now I'm wondering if you know Raymond Nolan's home
address...?" Perhaps by catching him away from the office and
the protective mounds of paper on his massive desk, I'd throw
him off guard and get him to open up to me.

"Don't you think it's dangerous to go to his house?" she
asked. "After all that's happened?"

"I have to see him. I can't let this go. Especially because of
what's happened. Look, I'm going there in broad daylight, and
you know where he lives. If you don't hear from me by this
afternoon, then you should call the police."

For a moment, the only sound between us was that of dead
silence. Then she said, "Raymond lives in one of the new
houses in Spencer Park. You can't miss them. There are only six
of them—brick, two-story homes. I was there last month to

discuss a fundraising event for the charity that's coming up this fall. You'll see his house as soon as you turn onto Spencer Court. It's the first one on the right, and he's installed "Save the People" posters on his front garden wall."

"Thanks. I'll talk to you later."

"Star, wait. Did Lorcan call you last night?"

"He called all right—he showed up here. Did you put him up to that visit?"

"I thought you might need some help. Did he do that?"

"Absolutely. Charming, like a prince. He'll probably tell you all about it when you see him. But I really have to go. Call you later."

I hung up and prepared for my trip to town. Lorcan and his promise to accompany me to the Garda Station came to mind. I'd have to get out of here soon, in case he arrived to make good on his part of the deal he'd made with O'Shea. I wanted to talk to Raymond before making any visits to the police. And I certainly didn't need Lorcan McHale to look out or make appointments for me.

I wrote a note saying that I'd gone into town and would be back soon. Then I stuck it on the kitchen door.

I smiled to myself as I relished Lorcan's dilemma when he got here and I was gone.

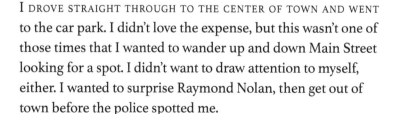

I DROVE STRAIGHT THROUGH TO THE CENTER OF TOWN AND WENT to the car park. I didn't love the expense, but this wasn't one of those times that I wanted to wander up and down Main Street looking for a spot. I didn't want to draw attention to myself, either. I wanted to surprise Raymond Nolan, then get out of town before the police spotted me.

I didn't notice anyone following me on the drive in. I assumed they would leave me alone until they figured out that I was a no-show for the little tea party they and Lorcan had planned. After locking the car and walking toward Main Street, I cut over to Castle Street, then Station Road to the Spencer Park development. It would take me twenty minutes on foot, but I'd be less conspicuous.

As I reached Main Street, the headlines on the newspaper stands outside Wynne's and Fahy's shops drew my eyes as if they were magnets.

DRUG DEATH CHALLENGES STEREOTYPES screamed the *Connaught Telegraph*. And WELL-MANNERED FINAN-CIAL INVESTMENT ADVISOR HAD ALL THE TRAPPINGS OF SUCCESS said *The Mayo News*.

Each featured head shots of Sharon. Probably from her work bio.

I stopped to read the articles. Both stated that she'd died of an apparent synthetic cocaine overdose. So her death was relegated to misguided experimentation with drugs. The end of the article mentioned Matthew's death and conjectured that their relationship was based on a mutual substance abuse problem. "Drugs kill people. That's the bottom line," one article ended with a quote from Detective O'Shea.

I couldn't believe any of this. How could the police be so stupid? What about the fact that Sharon had been strangled? How could they explain this situation away? How many more innocent victims had to die before the public protectors dropped their blinders and saw this for what it was?

Walking faster now, I went across Main Street to Spencer Park. Time was running out, and I had to find some answers.

∿

NOLAN'S RESIDENCE WAS A COLONIAL STYLE STRUCTURE WITH A bow window facing onto a spherical cul-de-sac. Several ancient chestnut trees formed a ring around a fountain in the middle of the circular turnaround. Gaslight lamps stood guard, lining the brick-paved driveways in the enclave of luxury homes. Heading up a charitable foundation must have its rewards, I thought. That's when I noticed two suitcases squatted in the driveway next to a Mercedes. It appeared as though I'd arrived just in time.

Nolan answered the door. Then, as he tried to close it in my face, he said, "I have no intention of talking to you today or ever."

"Do the police know about your trip?" I said, nodding toward the luggage.

"They have nothing to do with this," he shouted, then slammed the door so hard that it didn't catch, but flew open instead.

Since his back was turned to me as he walked away, I followed him down a narrow hallway into a brightly lit living room. I glanced around and saw no weapons, which was good. The furniture was covered with dust cloths, which told me he was planning an extended trip. Maybe he wasn't coming back at all. If that was the case, then this was my last chance to crack his shell.

He held himself erect, holding onto the right side of the fireplace's mahogany hearth. His face registered surprise when he finally noticed me.

"What the...."

"The door was open," I said. "So I assume you heard about Sharon."

"Yes, I have. I'm sorry she died. If only she'd listened to me, she—" Then he stopped in mid-sentence when he realized his slip.

Thank you, guardian angel, I whispered to myself. This is exactly what I'd hoped would happen.

"You're sorry?" I shot back. "That's all you have to say? The woman is dead and you're sorry? Don't you think you owe it to her to tell me what's going on? What did you tell her?"

Nolan flopped down into a chair, clutched his head in his hands, and rocked forward and backward. "I told her to get the hell away from Matthew. He was the source of her unhappiness. I'm sure of it. Going off all the time. A loner. Painting those pictures. Flirting with young girls who were influenced by his 'poor struggling artist' act."

His emotional outbreak, I had to admit, surprised me.

"Were you in love with her?" I asked. But I didn't need to hear his answer. The slump of his body in the chair and his purposeless agitation told their story.

"Yes, yes!" he shouted, pounding his head with his fists. "God damn her! God damn *me!* Yes! I've been in love with her for years. We were always together, the three of us. Sharon, Matthew, and myself. We used to joke about being the Three Musketeers. By the time I realized my feelings for her, she'd hooked up with Matthew."

"Didn't she know? Didn't you tell her how you felt? Did you even try?"

Anger and empathy surged through me. I let the anger take control. He'd allowed jealousy to eat away at him. And for that Sharon was dead.

"No. I hid it. I hoped she'd tire of Matthew. And then I'd be there to pick up the pieces." He sneered and laughed as if at himself or some bizarre joke. "I should have known that there's no kindness in this world. Time and again, I've had the life beaten out of me by fate."

As I listened to his words, a rush of emotions came to the surface. I let my anger toward him go at that moment, although a part of me didn't want to. I understood his losses—his dream of being a doctor, his sister, and now Sharon.... I've battled fate since I was six years old. But unlike Nolan, I wouldn't let it defeat me. Independence was my armor; information my weapon.

The flow of words ceased as he stared at the dark, cold fireplace. Immobile now, his rocking and head pounding ceased.

"What did you warn Sharon about?" I asked.

He looked up at me and then shrugged. "I guess it doesn't matter now. She came to me for help."

"What kind of help? Before Matthew died, or after?"

"She had a drug habit."

This wasn't exactly news to me. Or anyone else, for that matter, since every paper in town provided that information.

"What kind of help?" I asked again. "Did she want help quitting? Is that what she talked to you about?"

I had to keep him talking; he looked like he was in a catatonic stupor.

"She wanted Matthew off her back. He suspected her habit, but she never admitted it to him. Can you believe that? She was supposed to be in love with him, but she confided in me. How ironic. She asked me to help convince him that she didn't have a habit. She promised she'd quit if I'd buy her some time. She didn't want him asking questions and watching her every move."

"Did you agree to help her?"

"Of course. I had to be careful, though. I didn't want Matthew to know she'd told me her secret. Then I saw him with Skye, and I became suspicious of both of them. I didn't know what to believe. Maybe Matthew was supplying Sharon. Maybe Skye was. What if she'd lied to me about why she wanted Matthew off her back? Everything became very confusing. Then he died."

"How did Sharon act then?"

"Worse," he said. "I tried to see her. Call her. She refused me. I just wanted to help her. I loved her."

"And what about when I saw the two of you arguing on the street? What was that about?"

"More of the same. She looked terrible. I asked her to let me get her into rehab. She blew up and told me to mind my own business. And then you happened along."

He gave me an accusatory glare, but I've had a million of those aimed at me and was impervious.

"What do you think now? Do you still suspect Skye?"

"I don't know what to think anymore. And to tell you the truth, I just don't care. But if I were you, I'd pack my bags and get off this godforsaken island before you end up like Sharon. Now, you'll have to excuse me. I'm leaving." He got up quickly and escaped the room.

I followed him back out into the hallway. "Where are you going?"

"Away. The publicity about Matthew and Sharon is hurting the foundation." He turned back to me and added, "I've told the board of directors that I'm taking a leave of absence."

I studied his face carefully. The fine lines surrounding his eyes and lips were etched deep into his skin. He was paler and grayer than when I'd first met him. He looked tired and defeated, like he'd fought an unseen enemy for a long time and was now resigned to his fate as a loser.

I nodded without another word and walked out.

I didn't think I'd ever see Raymond Nolan again.

CHAPTER 22

Peter waited for me in front of French Hill cottage. While I parked my Renault, he jumped out of his own car, leaving the door open, and hurried over to me.

"Star, thank God you're back."

He pulled me close, his voice muffled as he spoke into my hair.

"I saw the papers. This place isn't safe, you're not safe. Have you been to the guards yet? Have you given up on this godforsaken wild goose chase?"

I pushed him away and pressed forward toward the cottage. I needed a few minutes to come to terms with the inner conflict I was experiencing—the surge of good feelings I felt when he pulled me toward him, in contrast to the anger with his attitude toward my involvement with the case.

By the time we reached the kitchen door, my emotions were more or less under control again.

"Come on in and I'll bring you up to date," I told him flatly.

I pointed to one of the kitchen chairs and turned to make tea. He offered to help, but I waved him off. Within minutes, I sliced some of Aunt Georgina's brown bread and had the tea, jam, and butter on the table. I played with the food on my plate while I considered where to begin. So much had happened in the last twenty-four hours.

"Well?" Peter prompted me.

"No, I haven't been to the police yet." I didn't tell him they were expecting to talk to me sometime that day.

"Why not? Don't you think you should tell them whatever you know and be done with this nonsense?"

I pushed my plate away. Why did everyone think I should run to the police? They hadn't done much so far other than bag the bodies and haul them off to the morgue. This morning's newspaper headlines proved how incompetent they were.

"I mean what do you know?" Peter said in response to my silence. "You've had a few conversations with Matthew's friends and it hasn't led anywhere. I don't understand why you don't just give your notes over to the guards and let it go at that."

He smiled and reached across the table to touch my hand. His charming manner was hard to ignore.

"Maybe you're right," I told him. Sometimes the best path is the path of least resistance. I didn't have the energy to explain to him that I don't let things go easily. "Everyone seems to have reached the same consensus."

"So why don't you join me on the island for the weekend?" Peter suggested, reaching across the table for a slice of bread.

I considered this invitation. It would give me an opportunity to get to know him better, and to visit the owner of the O'Malley pub as Richard had suggested. And the location of his lighthouse cottage would provide a great vantage point for trying to figure out Matthew's notes.

"You know, that's a great idea," I said. "I want to follow up on some information about my mother anyway."

"Okay, how about Friday evening? I'll pick you up when the Ocean Star docks."

I agreed, and then we sat quietly drinking our tea for a while. Peter talked about his recent commission to locate a set of 18th century diamond drop earrings, telling me what a rare find they happened to be.

"Antique earrings are the holy grail of the business," he explained. "And my client had a specific request for an elaborate centerpiece with three diamond drop pendants."

"Where did you find them?" I asked, curious about his contacts and resources.

"Oh, that's a trade secret, and I'm afraid I'd have to kill you if you knew about my sources," he replied, twisting his silver bracelet. "But I'd love to see them on *you.*"

"I'm afraid I've never been a proponent of the 'diamonds are a girl's best friend' philosophy." I was thinking about the diamond engagement ring Dylan had given me when he had asked me to spend the rest of my life with him. It could be described as modest at best—which had been fine with me.

"Just as well," Peter said. "They are rather fragile, and I wouldn't want something to happen to them before I delivered them to my client."

While we finished our tea, Peter related some of the strange situations he'd encountered in the antiquing business. When he left to attend a meeting he'd scheduled in Westport, I felt more relaxed, energetic, and ready to focus on the case again. So when I walked him out to the gate, I didn't hesitate.

"I'll see you on Friday," I said, and he seemed content with that.

I KNEW I HAD TO MAKE A FIRM DECISION ABOUT PETER ONE WAY or another. Did I really want to pursue what was obviously a romantic interest on his part? Was I even ready? It wasn't fair to welcome his visits and invitations if I wasn't.

The cottage's garden wrapped me in its serenity as I walked around smelling the roses and pondering my dilemma. Rose petals drifted from some of the blooms as I held them in my hand to enjoy their fragrance. My relationships, I have found, were as fragile as the roses that surrounded me. Is that why I was frightened about committing to Peter? Turning back toward the cottage, I reminded myself that I'd made a commitment to him about the weekend—and I meant to keep it.

Back inside, the spurt of energy I'd felt about the trip to Clare Island evaporated as soon as I saw my notes sitting on the kitchen counter. I'd dedicated my life's mission to using information and documentation to help people tell their stories or, at the very least, find the answers they needed. The emptiness and silence emanating from those notes weighed down on me, because the only story I had to tell for Matthew and Sharon at this point was about their death. But like all the commitments I make, I was willing to do whatever I could to fulfill them. I was still fully determined to find out what happened to Matthew and Sharon.

I took a look at my reflection in the mirror hanging over the mantel place and said, "Star, it's time to get help."

I decided then that I would go to the police in the morning and tell them everything I knew.

CHAPTER 23

The Castlebar police station was located in a new building that was adjacent to one of the oldest, the courthouse. It wasn't too many years ago that the people in the surrounding villages were making their own laws and dispensing their own justice.

Three policemen occupied the front reception area. One of them was seated behind a computer monitor. Looking up at me, he politely asked if he could help. A few minutes later I was waiting in Thomas O'Shea's office with a cup of tea in my hand.

O'Shea strutted into the room like a prizefighter who's just won his latest match. Keenan followed close on O'Shea's heels.

O'Shea smiled and said, "Lorcan isn't with you."

"No, I'm minding myself today. You look rather pleased with yourself. Have you found Sharon's killer?"

"I *am* pleased. The case is officially closed. In fact, we don't need to waste any more of your time. You are free to leave."

"The case is closed," I repeated like a person in a trance.

"Another drug overdose. These people take care of removing themselves eventually. But thanks for coming in," O'Shea said, then held the door open.

"But wasn't Sharon strangled?"

Leaving the door open, O'Shea sauntered over to his desk. His blue eyes shone cold and hard as he leaned toward me. "Ms. O'Brien, you're a visitor in this country. I don't mean to offend you, but I want to make it clear that your ideas and information are not wanted. They don't hold any weight here. This case—both of these cases—are *closed*."

Closed! I burrowed further into the chair, trying to understand his arrogance and total mishandling of these matters. Was he a crooked cop? Was it even possible he had something to do with Matthew and Sharon's untimely passing?

"But, she was choked to death," I told him. "I heard there was a nylon around her neck. How much more evidence do you need?"

"Like I said, Ms. O'Brien, this is a gardai matter. It's not for the likes of you, a foreigner, to question or even know the facts of the case." He shuffled some papers on his desk to make it clear I was nothing but a trivial distraction at the moment.

"I wasn't honest with you when we spoke," I continued. "I have information that may help identify Matthew's and probably Sharon's killer."

O'Shea took a long, deep breath and shifted his jaw slowly from right to left. "Like I said, the case is closed. Now if you'll excuse me, I have other work to do." He shuffled the papers some more.

I shifted my weight in the chair.

"Just like that? Two people's lives and reputations are destroyed. Their families are shocked, filled with grief and disbelief. Are you so heartless that you won't even listen to what I have to tell you?"

"You had that opportunity. You chose not to share it then. I choose not to hear it now." He gestured with his hand toward the door and the hallway beyond it. "Please enjoy the rest of your stay in Ireland. I understand we're in for a spell of dry weather."

"Matthew and Sharon were murdered—and I'll *prove* it." I rose from the chair, held my head as high as I could, and slammed his door behind me.

AFTER I HAD STOMPED THROUGH THE RECEPTION AREA AND BACK out to the sidewalk, a riot of colorful flowers on the green across the street caught my attention. A creative gardener had designed the flowerbeds to form the word Castlebar. Vibrant greens, yellows, purples, and whites...they were so beautifully alive. And so was I.

But not Sharon and Matthew.

Guilt clamped down on me. A lump in my throat obstructed my breathing. I reminded myself again that Sharon might have been killed because of my persistent search for the truth. The colors of those vibrant flowers, the relentless heat, and my equally relentless guilt swarmed my senses. Then my stomach contracted painfully and I heaved my breakfast onto the cement. Thankfully, no one was around to witness this.

Breathing as deeply as I could, I eyed the flowers yet again. Like a dose of smelling salts, they reminded me that I had work to do. In control again, I headed for the car.

IT DIDN'T TAKE ME LONG TO GET TO FRENCH HILL AND CALL Bridget. She agreed to let me see Matthew's house again. I picked up the key from her then drove toward Westport.

Cold, damp air enveloped me when I opened Matthew's door. (The walls of a house always seem to know when they no longer surround living, breathing people.) I didn't have any idea what to look for. Only my gut told me I needed to search Matthew's place again.

I began with his studio on the second floor. As I climbed the stairs, the cold air became frigid. My breath appeared before my eyes in puffs of steam. I buttoned my jacket, tugged a pair of gloves out of the pockets, and crammed my hands into them.

Slivers of dim light cut through the shuttered windows. I walked over to open them and noted the pier below. The sharp chill in the room contrasted with the pleasant scene of families strolling along the paths, pausing to look at boats, and keeping their children from getting too close to the edges. Then my eyes locked on someone who seemed to be looking directly at the window where I stood. The dark stocking cap did nothing to hide the blonde hair. It was Lucia! What was she doing here? When she realized I'd seen her, she turned away, thrusting her hands into her jacket pockets, hurrying toward the street.

I zoomed down the stairs and through the front door, but not before she vanished into thin air. I turned back to the apartment.

A deep silence pervaded every room as if listening expectantly for what I might find. I went straight into Matthew's studio. The unfinished drawing that had made me uneasy last time still stood on the easel. But his other art work was boxed and crated, waiting for his family to remove it and store it away in some dark corner of a room, attic, or basement. It struck me that his expressions of life wouldn't be revealed again until some other significant event like another death, move, or the need to make room for someone else's forgotten life. Matthew's art, like his soul, would essentially be buried for good. And his family would let go and continue with their lives.

I wondered why they had left this one painting uncrated. Remembering how different it had appeared from his other work, I studied it again, sizing up the painting's dark and warm reds, oranges, and yellows.

When I stepped forward to look at it in more detail, the picture's contents appeared to shift. So I stepped back and saw again the dark background of clouds and sky. I moved forward once more and noticed that the center and foreground clouds and sky were painted in lighter, cooler almost luminous blues and white. Maybe Matthew had been doing more than experimenting with a new technique. Maybe he had left a clue.

An article I'd read about Renaissance masters who had hidden things in their paintings came to mind. Did Matthew have similar intentions here? There were no faces evident in this particular work; at least none that I could see.

I stepped to and fro in the dimming light trying to discern what Matthew's message, if any, might have been. The colors in the middle of the picture were in perfect alignment, almost like a set of lanterns illuminating a path to the roiling turbulent darkness above. I went back to my car to find some paper and pencil. When I returned, I used the paper to trace the outline of the painting and write notes about the colors. I also took a picture with my cellphone to refer to later on, if need be.

When I went downstairs again it was notably warmer. Dust motes swirled in the air, cobwebs draped in corners, a fly buzzed against one of the windows. The furniture was huddled in the middle of each room, stripped of all adornments and waiting to leave.

At that moment, I was reminded of how hard it has always been for me to face changes in my personal life. Acceptance was the issue at hand. And my reluctance to accept what I cannot change spills all too often into my work life. Like an affectionate bulldog, I dig my teeth into something and work at it until I'm satisfied there's nothing left to do but let go. I'd wanted to do that for Matthew and Sharon. But as I stood in what was more like a tomb than a home, I realized there was nowhere else to go with this investigation. Maybe my idea about a clue hidden in the painting might be possible. But it was pretty thin compared to the other facts that supported

Matthew's guilt. I hated to admit it, but perhaps the police were correct in their conclusions.

I whispered a short prayer for both Matthew and Sharon, "Bless you," I said softly, "and know that I'm sorry that I couldn't change the outcomes."

I couldn't help wondering how many times I'd have to taste defeat in my life. Hope and certainty of my mother's love had sustained me thus far. But clues to her whereabouts were as sparse as the thin threads that dangled from Matthew's case. All the facts surrounding my mother's disappearance pointed to abandonment. All, that is, except for the one I held in my heart. I will never believe she deserted me willingly.

I turned out of the living room and headed toward the front door—and toward warmth, life, and moving on. Then, reaching for the handle, I noticed Matthew's mail resting on a cardboard box inside the front door. I hesitated for a moment, then gathered up the pile. It was comprised mostly of art catalogues and newsletters. They looked out of place here, colorful and lively, unlike the cold, dark hallway that was barely lit by the fading day.

I flicked automatically through everything. I stopped when I noticed that one of the pieces was addressed to Sharon. It was an antique-furniture newsletter called 'The Family Attic.' I turned it over and read the publisher's name—Scott Bell. It made sense to me that Sharon and Matthew would share some of the same interests. Since it was art and antiques in this instance, I wondered whether Peter knew Sharon. I made a mental note to ask him on Friday.

I took one last look around and then stepped outside, shutting the door firmly behind me.

∾

I HOUR. I'D FORGOTTEN THE SURGE OF TRAFFIC THAT FLOWS

through Westport in the late afternoon, as workers returned to villages like Belcarra and Turlough. While I sat in my car waiting for the traffic signal to turn green, I noticed the unmistakable stocking cap and blonde hair that flowed beneath it. Lucia emerged from the red door of Young's Interesting Books.

She wasn't getting away from me this time. As she moved along the crowded sidewalk, I edged my car out of the line of traffic and into a parking spot along the curb. Parking meter? Forget it. I'd chance the ticket rather than waste time digging for change.

Minutes later I came abreast of her.

"Lucia...." I gently nudged her elbow to get her attention.

Arms laden with painting books, she moved away from the curb toward one of the shop doors when she heard her name. Then, upon seeing me, her eyes widened and she pursed her lips.

"Oh, it's you," she said.

"I'm sorry if I frightened you. Were you expecting your mother or father?"

A red flush spread over her pale features, and her eyes widened even more. "Oh no, no. Not them."

"Then who, Lucia? I saw you back there at the apartment. Matthew's apartment. And I know you saw me. Why don't you tell me what's going on?"

She seemed reluctant to answer, so I looked around for somewhere we could talk privately. We were already standing in front of Curry's Cottage, a tiny tea shop and bakery.

"Why don't we have a cup of coffee?" I said, nodding toward Curry's green window sashes.

She nodded, shifting the books in her arms, and turned into Curry's narrow door. Then she walked toward an empty table and placed the books on a chair. I offered to get our drinks while she waited. She wanted a hot chocolate.

After a few minutes of warming our hands on the hot mugs

and taking our first careful sips, I asked again, "So why don't you tell me what's going on?"

She removed the stocking cap and pushed her blonde hair behind her ears.

"Nothing. Nothing is going on. Matthew promised to give me a book about the history of women and art. I don't know why, but I thought I might still get it. Perhaps his sister, umm...." Her voice faltered as the words ran out.

"What, Lucia? You thought his sister might be at the apartment?"

She shrugged. "I didn't know. I thought if I hung around I'd see someone. But then I saw you and I got scared." She punctuated the sentence with another shrug.

I sat back in my chair and pushed my mug away to the side to clear the space between us. "So what is it you're afraid of? What else do you know about Matthew, and what happened on Clare Island? You know that Sharon Dawson is dead, don't you?"

"Yes, I heard it on the radio. I can't. I don't know anything about it, though. She and Matthew fought a lot. That's all I know for certain. That and the fact that I just want to be an artist and get away from that island." Her eyes brimmed with tears as she looked away from me to her pile of books.

Was she telling me the truth, or was she putting on a dramatic act? Teenagers—it's hard to size them up. Their emotional range often changes within a few minutes.

I decided to treat her more like an adult than a teenager.

"Lucia, you realize that if you know anything, you're in danger. There's no doubt now with Sharon's death that there's a killer at work here. Don't you think it would be wise to tell someone if you have any knowledge about her and Matthew?" I paused, waiting for these ideas to sink in.

"I don't know any more than what I've already told you," she snapped back. Then she reached for the stocking cap and pulled it down over her hair again. "My parents don't want me speaking with you or anyone else about Matthew."

"Why not, Lucia? What are you hiding? Were you planning on meeting someone in Westport?" I had to rush my questions since she was obviously preparing to bolt.

She stood up, grabbed her books, and tossed some euros on the table. "I have to go or I'll miss the bus back to Roonagh Quay, and my parents will worry."

Her eyes pleaded with me, I noticed.

I nodded. I wasn't going to learn anymore from her now. I hoped to God she was telling the truth about not knowing anything further about Matthew and Sharon.

For her sake.

CHAPTER 24

I was home before I knew it. For once I didn't end up behind any tractors crawling along like a funeral procession. The sun sank into the horizon and the evening's calm descended like an Amen at the end of a prayer. So be it; I felt free. My shoulders lifted now that I'd made the decision that I'd done as much as I could for Bridget. Perhaps I'd get some peripheral information about the strange painting in Matthew's apartment, but nothing that would shed additional light regarding what really happened to him. At least I'd be able to report that he shared his artistic talents freely, and that they were appreciated and respected by someone with credentials like Richard O'Malley.

I also reminded myself that tomorrow would bring another day, and with it the promise of something new. I believe that every wall has a door. I began to think about my weekend with Peter, and I realized I was looking forward to spending more time with him. I also thought that there was still a chance I might learn something more about my mother.

I took my phone out and dialed Bridget's number. It went to her voicemail almost immediately.

"Bridget, this is Star O'Brien. I wanted to give you a status report, but I guess I've missed you. If you can, call me early tomorrow morning. Otherwise I'll be on Clare Island for the weekend."

Moments later I connected with Phillie.

"Sorry I haven't gotten back to you," I told her, "but with Matthew Sumner, the five-hour time difference, and lack of reliable electronic gadgetry at my fingertips, I'm a bit lost. Did you get the picture I emailed?"

"Yup." I heard a keyboard clattering in the background. "I've printed the picture you scanned and sent it along with your description to an art expert here in Ridgewood. It may be a day or two before he responds—there's an art show in town this weekend."

"Okay, call me with the results. I don't know when I'll be in the Internet Café to check emails again, so leave a message on my phone." It was midday Thursday in New Jersey, so maybe I'd hear something later tonight.

"Boss? You didn't call me back about the message I left you."

"I apologize for that, Phillie. Being three thousand miles away, I may as well be thirty thousand. What's going on?"

"You're not going to believe this, but our search software picked up an inquiry about a Maggie O'Malley. She was born around 1952 and grew up in Achill."

"Who made the inquiry?"

"She's near Castlebar. A village called Cong, in County Mayo. Her name is Evelyn Cosgrove." Phillie then recited the phone number. After that, I heard her say "Are you there?" just before I terminated the call.

Minutes passed. Water dripped from the kitchen faucet. A tractor rolled up the road. Everything seemed both normal and surreal to me. Was it coincidental that someone was looking for a woman with the same name as my mother? At least this Evelyn person didn't share the O'Malley surname! I knew I'd have to talk to her to determine, at the very least, if we were looking for the same Maggie.

Lots of unanswered questions....

I lifted the phone from its cradle and dialed. Then a recorded voice came on the line— "You've reached Evelyn Cosgrove. I'm out of the office on holidays, returning on September ten."

I ended the call and counted the days between now and the tenth. It was twenty-five...or a lifetime. I wondered which it would be.

When I heard the knock on the back door, I fully expected to see Aunt Georgina standing out there. When she doesn't hear from me for a day, she shows up at the cottage unannounced. But it wasn't her.

"I knew you'd return eventually," Lorcan said as he marched into the kitchen.

"What are you doing here?" My voice rasped in my throat as the day's annoyances and disappointments flooded into me. To emphasize this, I pointedly stared at my watch. "It's after nine thirty. Do you normally pay visits so late?"

"I think it's about time we talked about our relationship," he went on, ignoring my question. "From the moment we met, I've sensed that you didn't trust me. Don't deny it. I want an explanation. You owe it to me and to Dylan. He would have wanted us to be friends." Lorcan then walked into the living room and plunked himself into one of the armchairs.

Friends.... Is that really what Dylan would have wanted? I didn't think so. Suddenly all my feelings of grief about Dylan welled inside of me and burst out in the general direction of my latest guest.

I strode over to the other chair and sat down, grasping its

arms for support. "Dylan rarely talked about you other than to say you're trouble! Tell me how that adds ups to friendship?"

Lorcan's laughter roared through the cottage. "Trouble? Is that what he called me? Has that been the problem all along?" He paused, looked at my face, stopped chuckling, and continued. "I can see I need to explain."

Frustrated, tired, and feeling more fragile than ever, I could only nod.

He leaned forward, his eyes locked on mine. "Believe me when I tell you, there was nothing in it. Dylan and I really were friends."

"They why didn't he talk about you?"

Lorcan shifted his weight against the back of the chair as if bracing himself.

"We had a falling out a few years ago." He paused, repositioned his body, and took a deep breath. "Over you."

Over me?! I wanted to laugh out loud—now I'd heard it all.

"You didn't even know me, Lorcan!"

"No, I didn't. But Dylan was here on one of his flying visits. And he told me that he'd met someone he loved whose name was Star O'Brien." Lorcan clasped his hands in front of him, leaned further over the edge of the cushion, and began quoting Dylan. "'Lorcan,' he said, 'I've fallen hard. She's had a bit of bother in her life, making her fiercely independent. She's lost everyone she's loved. But she's lost, too, trying to find her mother. I don't know if she'll have me, but I'm going to try like hell. At whatever cost.'"

Lost? Could Dylan really have said that? Is that what he thought?

"But why didn't he tell me about this place?" I demanded. "Or about you or Aunt Georgina?" I didn't think I could bear to hear his answer—but at the same time, I had to know.

Lorcan sighed. "Her name was Caitlin May."

I stared at Lorcan's fingers, watching them pale to a bloodless pallor, as he girded his hands against the arms of the chair.

"I don't understand...who's Caitlin May?"

"*Was*, Star. She's dead." Lorcan's chest heaved as he expelled a heavy breath. "She and Dylan lived together for several years. They met when he was on one of his business trips and he'd stopped here for a few days."

I didn't move. I didn't breathe. I focused on Lorcan's white knuckles and wondered if I could hold on to my sanity like that. Dylan had been my rock, and our love was the foundation of my life. My soul quaked as the meaning behind Lorcan's revelation rolled over me.

"Ten years his junior and a dedicated botanical researcher, she didn't mind his frequent business trips." Lorcan stopped here, shook his head, and focused his gaze at the stone-cold fireplace grate before continuing. "It happened quickly. She contracted a virus during an experiment and was dead within hours." He stood up and began pacing around the room. "Dylan was devastated. Swore he'd never love anyone again. And then he met you. He struggled with telling you about Caitlin. We discussed it and I urged him to tell you about his past. But he wanted a clean break. So he decided to keep the Irish part of his life a secret." Lorcan threw himself back into the chair and gazed into my eyes. "He didn't want to expose you to his pain, or jeopardize his relationship with you." When I didn't respond to this, he continued with, "He also didn't want you to waste your time looking for your mother." At this he shrugged and sighed. "I don't know, Star.... I don't know."

"Don't stop." I told him. "I want to hear it all."

"Sure, okay. He was worried about your obsession with finding your mother. He believed that you had been abandoned, and he wanted to spare you the heartbreak of learning the truth. I think he wanted to make sure your relationship was based on love for each other, without any attachments, I guess he thought he'd have more time to tell you about here...."

Lorcan sighed again, pushing himself forward on the chair, and reached over to take one of my hands. But I refused his gesture, moving my own hands into my lap, where I folded them together to give myself support. How could Dylan have been so misguided? I wondered. And so arrogant that he thought he knew what was best for me?

"Star, I didn't agree with him and I told him so. That disagreement became so heated that it ended our friendship—and I never heard from him again."

Lorcan's words paralyzed me as if I'd been tasered.

He stood up, lowered his head, and said "I'm sorry, Star. Sometimes it's the people we love the most who bring us the greatest pain. I only wish to God I could turn back the clock and put him in this room with us now. I didn't want it to turn out like this...for any of us."

I nodded and watched him leave. Then I sat there for a long while. The clock ticked, a dog barked, and a lone car rumbled down the road.

Finally, I rose, turned out the lights, and went to bed.

CHAPTER 25

The next morning, the radio promised several days of beautiful weather with temperatures in the seventies. But no amount of sunshine could dispel my dark mood. I hadn't slept much, thinking about Dylan and our life together.

Isn't it ironic? Here I was in Ireland without him, and the very secrets he'd thought to keep from me were now ripped open. *Secrets....* Some people say that everyone keeps secrets. But how many is too many? And how do we keep our secrets from destroying other people's lives? Matthew had kept secrets from his sister, and now he was dead. Sharon too had kept secrets—I was sure of it—and she was also dead. Dylan's secrets had been hiding in a country three thousand miles away from where we existed in the United States. I wondered what other secrets the future held as I rolled up into a ball, pulled the covers over my head, and cried. I mourned for Dylan and what we'd had together—and what we'd missed because of his damn secrets.

ⁿN I HEARD THE BANGING ON THE BACK DOOR; I IGNORED IT,

thinking it might be Lorcan again. But it wouldn't stop. I knew then that it was Aunt Georgina.

When I opened the door a few moments later, she swept into the room and pulled me into a huge hug. Tears spilled down my face as she rocked me back and forth like a mother lulling its child to peaceful sleep. Finally, she held me at arm's length and said, "I don't know what was wrong with that nephew of mine."

She sat me down at the table and busied herself with filling the kettle and setting it on the stove to boil.

"Did you know?" I asked. Suddenly it was important for me to know if she had been part of decisions that Dylan had made.

She balanced herself on the chair opposite me. "I never knew about you until Dylan died."

I nodded. "It's okay, Aunt Georgina. I don't blame you for keeping his secrets."

"Now you listen to me Star O'Brien. I didn't know about you until Dylan had his heart attack. He was a wee lad, just four years old, when his mother—my sister—went to the States." At that moment, it struck me that Dylan hadn't ever said much about his parents. Just that they were deceased.

"She embraced her life there completely," Georgina went on, "and never crossed the Atlantic again. Once Dylan became a teenager, she'd send him to Ireland in the summer to visit my mother—his grandmother—in this house. Even though my sister hated the wet weather and the poverty she left behind, I think she wanted him to understand where he'd come from. I'd see him briefly when he'd arrive, but I never took too much notice of him otherwise. I was busy living my own life. Then, when he began his import business, he'd stop here once in a while for a day or two."

The kettle's whistle pierced the air. Aunt Georgina stood and made two cups of steaming tea. She pressed one of the mugs, which held a peppermint tea bag, between my hands.

"You didn't notice that he'd stopped coming here?!" I shook my head in disbelief. "That doesn't sound like you. You know everything there is to know about the comings and goings in this county." I blew on my tea and watched for her reaction.

"Well, I didn't know about *that!* Dylan arrived here on one of his whirlwind visits about five years ago and let me know that his business had grown so much that he couldn't take time to mind the cottage any more. Said he'd hired John Barrett to take care of the place, mow the lawn, and get someone in to dust. So other than a card at the holidays saying all was well and see you soon, he dropped off my radar."

She reached across the table and took my hands in hers.

"Believe me when I tell you, I didn't know about you until a solicitor contacted us to say that Dylan had died, and you would be coming here to settle his estate."

"But why didn't you say anything when you met me?"

"About what? All I knew was that you'd been named executor of his estate. And when I met you and saw how fragile you were with grief for Dylan, I didn't want to add to your burden by asking you why Dylan never introduced you to his friends and families." Aunt Georgina moved her cup around on the table. "Believe me. I didn't know. And I wouldn't do anything to hurt you Star."

Belief.... I took heart from Aunt Georgina's words. I'd gotten accustomed to her whirlwind arrivals and departures and her concern for me. I couldn't bear it if I lost her too.

"Drink some tea before it goes cold," she said. I nodded and took a sip while I studied the hazel trees through the kitchen window.

"What about Lorcan?" I asked. "Do you trust him?"

"Of course I trust him. When he called me this morning, he was concerned about you. He told me the whole story." She shook her head, threw the ends of her scarf back behind her ~~ lders, and leaned forward. "I always assumed that he never mentioned Dylan for the same reason I didn't—because Dylan was out of sight and therefore out of mind. Now that I know what happened, I see the last five years very differently. Yes, I believe Lorcan when he says that he and Dylan had a falling out." She shook her head again. "Humph, more silly behavior. Isn't it interesting how one action, one relationship can haunt us for our entire life?"

She paused here, then looked directly into my eyes.

"Star, I know you do everything you can not to show how fragile you are. This has all been a terrible shock for you, of course. But I also know that underneath this hurt and grief is a strong, brave, and independent woman. She's the one to nurture."

I shook my head slowly in agreement, stood up, and leaned over to give her a kiss on the cheek.

"Thank you, Aunt Georgina."

"Of course," she said. Then she glanced at her watch, jumped up from the chair, and straightened her scarf, "Now, I have a client meeting me at the shop this morning, so I have to run. Don't forget what I said." And with that she was out the door and up the road.

As I watched her walk away, I wanted to pull open the door, run after her, and beg for a hug. Instead, I threw myself on the love seat and wrapped my arms around my shaking body. What would my life have been like if my mother hadn't disappeared? For one thing, I doubt I would have made information brokering my life's work. Nor would I have met Dylan or the O'Brien's. And I certainly wouldn't be lying in French Hill cottage mourning the Dylan I'd known. In my gut, I knew that he loved me despite the secrets. My work has taught me that sometimes we have to accept the path that our choices puts us on. I've also learned that not every loving intention is pure.

What would life have been like?

THE TELEPHONE YANKED ME OUT OF MY REVERIE.

"Is this Brenda Starr, the Irish colleen?"

Although Jim Hipple was born, raised, and plodded his beat in the Bronx and had never set foot in Ireland, the retired cop did a decent Irish accent.

"Go away," I said into the phone, remembering how Jim began calling me Brenda Starr when he learned my first name. "I'm not in the mood for jokes at the moment."

"Well, you called love, and I've got the information you wanted. It's now or never."

Jim's threat reminded me of our relationship's many ups and downs. After leaving the force, he moved to Ridgewood and founded All Towns Investigations, Inc. The police were inept as far as I was concerned. But in my business, an information broker sometimes needs to be friends with a cop or at least be able to access police information. A retired cop turned licensed private investigator was as close as I'd gotten to making nice with the establishment.

"Okay," I sighed. "What did you find out?"

"I spoke to one of my many sources," Jim began. Then he paused, I was sure, to wait for my compliments on his resourcefulness. When silence ensued instead, he continued with "And I got connected to a coroner in Dublin. I'm afraid my dear that the cops are following protocol. When a small amount of narcotics are found on a body, it's put down to low-level drug use. With the focus on terrorism and other larger crimes, something like this gets closed immediately. Not enough manpower. Same with the girl, I think you said her name was Shar—"

"But," I interrupted, "the neighbors said she had a nylon wrapped around her neck. I don't know if that's true. It may just ssip." I glanced around the kitchen looking for my iPhone;

anything I could use to connect to a world that made sense. "I'm inclined to think she was murdered."

"Or, she got high and decided to take the easy way out."

"Everyone is giving up on Matthew and Sharon, as a matter of protocol!" I shot back, barely able to contain my frustration at how worthless the police could be.

"Doesn't matter, Brenda. Addicts, especially dead ones, don't deserve investigative attention. Drugs in the bloodstream make it an open-and-shut case. Now if you don't mind, I've got a surveillance to get to this afternoon. Catch you soon, Brenda."

He laughed and then was gone in an instant.

Glancing at my watch, I saw that it was now after three. Jim's call had forced me off the couch where I'd slept fitfully since Aunt Georgina's visit. Still in my pajamas, I tidied up the kitchen, boiled more water, and made a mug of tea. I didn't care about eating anything or getting dressed. I just didn't care.

With the tea in my hand, I wandered through the cottage, looking at the old furniture and pictures that had been in Dylan's family for a few generations. Still undecided about selling the property, I'd also left decisions about the contents to a later date. As I touched one of the antique Victorian kerosene lamps, I realized I yearned for the sense of security and continuity Dylan's family artifacts had provided.

Security....

Is that what I wanted? I thought about the call from Jim Hipple. I admitted to myself that sometimes we can't help but depend on other people for security. Matthew depended on his relationship with his sister, and where did that get him in the end? Bridget had depended on the police, and they had let her down. And after losing my mother and the O'Brien's, I'd grown to believe that my relationship with Dylan would provide me with lifetime security.

I caught a glimpse of the red eyes and pale face that looked back at me from the mirror over the fireplace. Then the phone in the kitchen began ringing. As I went to answer it, I remembered Aunt Georgina's advice and mentally agreed with her that I needed to reconnect with my inner strength.

I'd expected the call to be from Bridget, but was surprised to hear Peter's voice instead.

"I know we'll see each other tomorrow evening," he said, "but I couldn't wait 'til then. I wanted to see how your day went."

"All is well here." The lie came easily to my lips. I'd had enough soul-searching discussions with other people for a while. "In fact, I'm waiting for a call from Bridget. Do you mind if we catch up later?" It was true, I needed to speak with Bridget. But I also just didn't feel like talking to Peter.

"Well, okay." Peter paused before continuing. "You sound like there's something wrong. Has anything happened?"

The events of the last twenty-four hours flashed before my eyes as I twisted the phone cord and considered my answer. "Nothing's wrong," I lied, "but I'm wondering about this weekend. I'm not sure where our relationship is going—"

"Star, Star...wait a minute I thought our relationship's been fine. I haven't rushed you have I? I know you're getting over Dylan...."

"Peter, it has nothing to do with you. I need some time to myself, to think about the future, what I'm doing with this place, my mother.... There's just too much right now, and I don't need to complicate things further. Plus, I have a business to run in the States. I don't want to mislead you or waste your time, so I think it's best to forget this weekend."

"Star, will you stop worrying about me? I know how vulnerable you are. You need friends right now, and I want to be one of them, that's all. Why not come out to the island for the weekend? You can forget about your phone, take some walks, and go home on Monday with a fresh outlook. A few days rest, and
ll have everything sorted out. How about it?"

Fresh outlook.... As my eyes scanned the kitchen, the old family pictures, and pine antiques that decorated the room, I realized that a different perspective sounded inviting.

"Fine, okay. But don't think I'm going to be good company. You realize that, right?"

Peter laughed, "Relax. I'll see you tomorrow."

ALMOST IMMEDIATELY, THE PHONE RANG AGAIN.

"Star, this is Bridget Sumner. Sorry I hadn't gotten back to you, but I've been in meetings all day. What's going on?"

Her clipped, efficient tone struck a stark contrast to the weariness I'd heard in her voice the last time we spoke.

"I'm sorry to tell you this, Bridget," I began, "but there's not much more I can do. I have a few feelers out about the painting, but otherwise I've hit a wall. And whatever my contact says about it, it's likely not going to make a difference. Sometimes we have to take what we know and make sense and peace out of it. I'm sorry." I toyed with the telephone cord again, noticing that it was beginning to lose its shape from all the tension.

"Tell that to my parents, Ms. O'Brien," Bridget replied. "It breaks my heart to see them every day. I don't know how to give them closure. If only my brother had fit into the family business, he might still be alive."

"I'm sorry, Bridget, I really am."

We wrapped up our call with more thank-you's and pleasantries about my sojourn in Ireland.

Afterward, I thought about one word that she used in particular—closure. I knew all too well how Matthew's parents felt. Everyone who grieves searches for an end.

I looked around the room and headed to bed. This was one day that I wouldn't mind ending.

CHAPTER 26

I packed light, deciding to take the bus instead of my car to Roonagh Quay. That would give me a chance to be a true tourist.

After I'd deposited my car into the parking lot behind The Golden Thread, I threw my overnight bag over my shoulder and headed toward the door.

"Anyone home?" I asked, leaning in.

Aunt Georgina danced out from behind her cash register. This morning she wore an olive-green mid-calf length silk skirt with a boxy purple chenille sweater.

"Where are you off to this morning? I didn't expect to hear from you until later."

"I'm off to Clare Island for the weekend."

"Really? More research on Matthew?"

Her head tilted to the side as she asked this question. I watched her eyes move from me to the bag.

"No, I can't do anything more to help Bridget. There are some minor updates that she might want to hear, but nothing meaningful. You know I don't want to, but I must put this behind me, Aunt Georgina." Then I explained about my ting with the police and my visit to Matthew's house in

Westport. "I've already called Bridget and explained the situation to her."

"You really have had a bad few days, haven't you, love? But I'm relieved about your decision, Star. God knows what's really going on, but you can't solve it. I guess this will always be a mystery, something for people to gossip about."

"Probably," I said. "Anyway, I'll be staying with Peter. Here's his number in case you need to reach me." I handed her a piece of paper.

She glanced at it before turning her eyes back to me. "Don't tell me any more about Peter or anyone else for that matter. I've wished you and Lorcan would get to know each other better. You haven't really given him a chance, Star. Why you and he can't—"

"Sorry, I've got to run, Aunt Georgina. I see my bus pulling up across the street at Flannelly's Pub."

I gave her a quick smile and dashed away.

THE BUS LUMBERED ITS WAY ALONG THE NARROW AND TWISTING roads that sprawled at the feet of the Connemara Mountains. Or the 'Twelve Pins' as they are called locally.

After spending several hours sitting on my duff, I looked forward to the walk to the lighthouse. There was still time before the ferry arrived, so I decided to explore the quay. The last time I was here, I'd been focused on the Sumners' boat slip.

A young boy—about ten or eleven years old, blonde, and wearing a broad smile—manned the ticket office. I paid my fare and walked along the concrete wharf, stopping to watch a young cormorant spread its wings as it roosted on a small point of rocks rising out of Clew Bay. Although I wasn't following up on Matthew anymore, I couldn't help but look over to the Sumners' slip again. It was empty. Maybe Bridget or her parents had taken the boat out for the evening. Something to shift their minds away from their grief for a while.

As my eyes followed an imaginary line from their slip to the ocean, I glimpsed the back of a head that looked familiar. Was it Lorcan McHale talking to another man in the marina? With the sun shining between us, it was difficult to be sure. I squinted and used my hand as a shield, but then the two of them walked away.

The thought of seeing Lorcan brought back our recent conversation. Determined to forget about both, however, I plunked myself down on a large rock, periodically glancing out to the water where the *Ocean Star* wended its way to the pier. As it got nearer, more people joined me in watching its arrival. Most of them carried knapsacks, some picnic baskets. I wondered what it was like to live so close to the ocean and to these islands, the freedom of getting away to one of the cleanest beaches in Europe whenever the urge struck.

As my gaze fell on the group of people surrounding me, a ripple of shock electrified my spine. Raymond Nolan had stationed himself a little to my left, and he was glaring at me. The same bags that I had seen him posit into his car several days before lay on the ground at his feet.

Recovering from my initial surprise, I began moving in his direction. Where had he been since I last saw him? He looked tired, hadn't shaved in days, and was wearing the same clothes I'd seen him in at his house.

I was about to start firing questions when a black Labrador bounded between us. A bearded man scrambled over, trailing a leash in his hand and calling, "Wolf, get back here!" Then the man smiled at me. "Don't worry, he's friendly." I held myself still, watching as he reached down to grasp the dog's collar.

I began to circumvent the master-and-canine combo, but earded man mistakenly misread my movement as an indication that I wanted to pet his companion. So he led the dog over to me and said, "Go ahead, he likes to be petted."

Not wanting to appear rude, I reached down and rubbed Wolf under his chin. At the same time, I saw Nolan pick up his bags and walk over to the *Ocean Star* dock. Why was he going to Clare Island? Did he need to do something or see someone? If he was the murderer, then he might want to drop off some incriminating evidence. Or perhaps he had an accomplice waiting for him?

When I reached the boarding area a few minutes later, about twenty people stood in line in front of me. I watched Nolan, who was way ahead by now, descend the narrow set of stone steps and onto the boat. I waited for what seemed like an eternity before my turn to board. There wasn't much room left and I had no choice but to sit in one of the few remaining seats. That meant I was nowhere near Nolan. I satisfied myself with the knowledge that having been the first on, he'd be the last off. So I'd wait for him to disembark on the other side.

In the meantime, I busied myself gazing across the vast expanse of water that stretched to the Atlantic Ocean. The air felt cool, the breeze washed through my hair, the waves rocked the boat rhythmically. I imagined that I was listening to the soft strings of an Irish violin, its music drifting across the waves and wafting through my head. Songs from my ancestors, perhaps? Songs from my secret past, waiting for me to uncover them? Soon the twilight would descend, bringing with it the mysterious pull of haunting music and the need to finally solve the riddle of who my mother had been. We all have a secret past. Like a secret garden, it waits for us. In moments of contemplation, we go there in search of answers. Perhaps this trip would bring them to me.

I closed my eyes and savored these thoughts for the remainder of the journey.

When I opened my eyes again, the sky over the island had

turned dark and ominous. It reminded me of Matthew's strange painting. I took the tracing that I'd made out of my jacket pocket where I'd stuffed it after I'd emailed a scanned copy to Phillie. While I alternately stared at the dark sky before me and the picture in front of me, I caught a glimpse of Captain O'Malley in his cockpit successively scanning the horizon in front of him and the colorful outline of the topography of the island. In that moment it struck me that, like Lego pieces snapping together, Clare Island's outline and its coves fit the shape created by the roiling dark clouds and sky in Matthew's painting. In contrast, the painting's lighter section revealed a path across the middle of the island.

So maybe he *had* left a message! But what did it mean? Had Matthew hidden something on the island? Did his killer live on the island? My mind swirled with possibilities—and reawakened my determination to figure out what he tried to say.

UPON ARRIVAL, THE USUAL JUMBLE OF BODIES AND THEIR belongings progressed from the boat to the concrete dock. I waited for Nolan, never letting my eyes stray from his movements. Imagine my surprise when I then noticed Richard O'Malley disembarking with everyone else. I hadn't seen him on the boat and might have missed him entirely, but he paused for a moment—slinging his bulging army knapsack over his right shoulder—and this single action caught my eye. I waved to get his attention, but after nodding at me, he purposely kept his eyes focused on the ground and strode out of the area.

As the crowd on the dock thinned, I realized Peter wasn't there to meet me. Mist hung in the air like a gauzy veil, and I worried lest Nolan disappear as unexpectedly as he had appeared. But he didn't try to avoid me this time. Instead, he :hed directly to me.

"Can I help you with anything, Miss O'Brien?"

"You can tell me what you're doing here," I replied.

"Probably heading to the fires of hell." His ragged breathing interrupted the flow of his words. Up close, the black rings under his eyes looked like a grotesque application of eye liner. Shifting his weight from leg to leg, he continued. "Let's get off this cold concrete. I've got a car here. I can give you a lift to wherever you're going." He laughed as if he had insights to a private joke.

I quickly assessed my situation. I was by myself, with the ground fog rising and a long walk to the lighthouse ahead of me. I accepted, thinking it was better to keep him where I could see him. Besides, Peter would be at the lighthouse, so I wouldn't be alone with Nolan at the top of the mountain.

He scooped up my bag, and we crossed the dock and beach area. Then into the parking lot, where we halted at an older model Volkswagen Beetle with the steering wheel on the left side. Before I could ask the question, he said, "I bought it from an American artist who used to live in the lighthouse. I've never taken it off the island. It's handy transportation whenever I'm here."

"Are you here that often?" I asked, easing myself into the passenger seat.

"Often enough."

"What are you doing here now?"

"I need to get away for a few days, as I told you before. This is as good a place to do that as any other. Better even, because of the solitude." He started the engine and backed out of the parking lot. "Where are you going?"

"I'm on my way to the lighthouse cottages," I said. "Do you know where they are?"

"I do," he said and steered the car in their general direction. "Do you mind my asking why you are going there?"

"I'm spending the weekend with a friend of mine."

"The American? The one who's got the antiques business?" His voice rose an octave in his surprise.

"Yes, what about it?"

"Nothing," he said. I could sense his usual brusque tone in his reply. "It's only that I've never heard of him being friendly with anyone. He has a reputation for being reclusive. Lives behind gates and walls."

I nodded but didn't really want to debate this point with him. "What about you?" I asked. "Where are you staying?" With the clues that Matthew's painting had provided about the island, I wanted to know if Nolan lived near the island's center line.

"Up the hill here a bit. My family owns a small cottage there. We use it for weekend getaways."

"Were you on the island that weekend?

He glowered at me and shrugged his shoulders as if he didn't know what my question meant.

"You know," I continued, "the weekend that Matthew's body was found." I watched his face carefully.

He kept his head turned toward the road, shifting his body so that he was sitting up higher. His hands tensed on the wheel, turning his knuckles white.

"I've told you before, I had nothing to do with Matthew's death. I really don't want to get into discussing it again."

We rode in silence for a short time after that. Then he pointed and said, "Okay, there's the lighthouse. I'll drop you at the gate." A moment later he did so, adding, "Enjoy whatever time you have here, Ms. O'Brien."

I got out, retrieved my bag from the back seat, and thanked him. Then I stood there watching the taillights of his car fade away below me.

≈

I GULPED AIR TO STEADY MY NERVES. BEING CONFINED IN THE CAR with him for those few moments, I'd seen his personality swing from desperation to cool rage. Was his anger about Sharon's death or was it because I'd shown up on the island? Maybe both...or perhaps something else altogether.

The air that touched my skin had become colder and damper. Twilight had descended into darkness, I turned and continued on to the gate, only to find it locked. There weren't any lights on in the cottage. Funny, I'd expected Peter to be here to meet me.

I deposited my bag there and climbed up the hill even further, to the edge of the cliff. Up here, the wind whipped my hair into a froth. An inky darkness absorbed any light that might have provided reflection, and as white capped waves crashed onto the rocks below me, the ocean stretched infinitely. I struggled with the awe of standing at the last point of land overlooking the Atlantic Ocean. There was real terror in knowing that the slightest wrong movement would send me tumbling over the edge, plummeting about four hundred feet to my death with the sound of the gulls cawing in my ears. I imagined Grace O'Malley standing here and understood the power she must have sensed with the world at her feet. I was completely alone on this wild outcrop, as she may have been many times.

I swayed, suddenly dizzy with my imagination and the height, as I felt drawn to the magnetic pull of the ocean's waves.

"Hello, who's that?"

The words came out of the mist almost at my back. I jumped, losing my balance, and fell to my knees. I grabbed the ground around me to steady myself and keep from rolling forward. My body shook uncontrollably with the realization that my fear had almost become a reality.

"Star, is that you?" Peter's voice sounded above me, and I felt a firm hand pull me to my feet. "Are you all right? You could have been killed." He took my hand and began leading me toward the cottage.

"You gave me such a fright. Your voice...." I didn't finish because he hushed my words by covering my mouth with his. I responded with equal fervor, a hot twinge of longing circulating through every part of my body.

When we finished, he said, "Come inside. I've been waiting for you."

CHAPTER 27

When we stepped over the threshold of his cottage, I understood why I hadn't seen any lights. Candles danced, casting shadows into every corner, like the entrance to a dark and mysterious forest in the twilight hours.

I savored the notion that Peter and I would uncover these mysteries together, perhaps tonight. He kissed me again. I kissed back and allowed my body to mold itself into his. With a mumbled groan, he placed his arms on mine and disentangled himself.

"Star, come into my kitchen and keep me company while I prepare this feast."

I followed him toward a large room in the back that ran the width of the cottage. When he turned on the lights, I saw that half of the kitchen reflected its original state, complete with an open hearth, while modern appliances occupied the other half.

He led me to a rocking chair in front of the hearth and told me to relax while he got dinner ready. A small turf fire twinkled in the grate. As I fell into the rocking motion of the chair and gazed into the light of the fire, the sounds of Peter's movements faded. "You can make the salad now," he said, his voice bringing me back to the present. He'd assembled all the fixings on one of the counters, so all I had to do was toss them together and add the Caesar dressing.

As Peter worked, he moved slowly and calmly, and I felt my body relax even further into the warmth of the kitchen and the smells of the food. He removed two small steaks from the grill and arranged them on dinner plates. With a flourish, he balanced both plates on his hands, suspended high over his head.

"If my lady will follow me, please."

I grabbed the salad and followed him into the dining room. It was bathed in candlelight coming from small votive candles that covered the farmhouse-style table. There was also a clean, airy simplicity here. The only furniture consisted of the dining table and six chairs, and each wall hosted just one painting.

Peter placed our plates on the table and guided me into one of the ladder-backed Shaker chairs.

"This room is beautiful," I said. "Is this set one of your antique finds?"

"No, they're reproductions. I special ordered them to fit the dimensions of this room and asked the workmen to distress the finish."

While we ate, we talked more about his work. He told me stories of furniture that he'd found in barns and sheds that turned out to be valuable collector's pieces. Listening to him made me remember the antiques newsletter that Sharon subscribed to. I tugged it out of the back pocket of my Capris and set it on the table.

"Peter, are you familiar with this newsletter? It's called 'The Family Attic.'"

"Why, yes. It's got a small following, mostly people who like to find family treasures hidden among the junk. I know Scott Bell, the editor, as I've contributed several articles about family ooms that people may not realize are valuable." His eyebrows went up as he glanced from the newsletter back to me. "Why do you ask?"

"Well, I found a copy at Matthew Sumner's place. It's addressed to Sharon and—"

"Star, more of this obsession with Sumner? Tonight?" His voice was so low that I could hardly hear him. "I thought you were going to give everything a rest this weekend. Can't you let Matthew rest in peace? He's dead. We're alive." Then he added, "I thought we would give ourselves a chance to explore our friendship over the next two days."

"I only considered it because you talked about finding treasures in barns and sheds. With your involvement in the antiques trade, your newsletter, and your proximity to Matthew when he lived on the island...well, I thought that you might remember seeing Matthew and Sharon at an antique show. Or maybe they subscribed to your newsletter, too."

"Enough," Peter said as he rose out of his chair. "You'll never let this rest, will you?"

I rose also, reaching my hand out to him. "Peter, it's only a question. Why are you getting so upset?"

He looked at me and shrugged.

"It's because I'm concerned for you and I'm worried sick that you'll be hurt or even killed." Then, his voice rising again, he added. "For God's sake, Star, this is not a game."

I took a step away from him, and when he spoke again his voice was almost a whisper.

"Can't you see how fond I am of you? Perhaps more than fond. I want you to focus on us, not other people, especially not dead people. I know you've suffered losses—your lover, your parents. But that's the past. You're here now, and I want you with me."

His words came as if from far away, and suddenly I felt as though I was in a fog or the clouds. My head spun, and the candlelight flickers made the shadows dance a jig.

I took another step back.

"I want to leave, now," I said, turning toward to the door. Then Peter grabbed my hand and pulled me back to him.

"Look, Star, I'm sorry. Please stay. You're just tired."

"It's okay," I said, pushing him away. "I understand your anger. And you're right, I'm tired. A little confused, too. I think I'd like to walk back to the hotel and call it a night."

"If that's what you want, let me drive you down there."

"No, I need the fresh air." I stammered over my words as I stumbled out of the dining room. "Tomorrow's another day, Peter. I'll call you in the morning."

I opened the front door and left.

CHAPTER 28

S hivering, I cursed myself for leaving my jacket at Peter's place. High above me, the stars shone like cold diamonds. No warmth there. Cloud cover momentarily hid the full moon, making it seem dull and smaller than usual barely lighting the narrow path down toward the harbor.

As the wet grass soaked my feet inside my sneakers, I realized that power walking was out of the question. I picked my way slowly along the grassy slope, dodging the pieces of stone and pebbles and the sheep dotting the grassy landscape that I could make out in the dim moonlight. One false step and I'd be on my behind again like earlier in the week. But this time I might not be so lucky to only twist my ankle.

I glanced back at the lighthouse and wondered if I should ask Peter to drive me down to the bay after all. Then I saw that the lights were all out now. I weighed my options and decided it was better to continue down instead of venturing back.

I stood still for a few minutes, trying to visualize the path that I'd taken several times in the past when I'd hiked to the harbor in daylight. At the same time, I replayed my conversation with Peter. Why was I so sensitive? Why was I running away like this? What was I running away from? It certainly

wasn't Peter. I realized that it was me, and perhaps more importantly that the ability to move into the future was in my hands.
I'd already experienced so much sadness, I wondered if I could
face anymore.

I had to admit that Peter was right about one thing. I
needed to make room for someone else in my life again. I
couldn't mourn Dylan forever. Life is for the living. I imagined
what it would be like to have someone to snuggle up to at night
—to share my dreams about finding my mother, to confide my
deepest fears. I'd never know if I didn't give Peter a chance—
and if I didn't let Dylan go and give myself a chance.

In the instant I realized that I'd have to turn around, a pair
of arms encircled me and Peter's voice whispered in my ear.

"I can't let you go like this, Star."

I leaned back into his body, twisted my head, and looked up
into his eyes.

"I know what you're thinking. I've been thinking ...."

The flow of words halted as the moonlight reappeared from
behind its cover to reveal the hypodermic needle that Peter
wielded in his right hand.

"That's been your problem all along—you think too much."

His left arm wrapped itself around me tighter as he poised
the needle above my right.

"Oh my God, you? *You're* Matthew's killer?!"

I formed these words instinctively. The realization of where
we stood and how alone we were gripped my stomach with a
sickening dull ache.

He shoved me around so that he stood opposite to me. The
hypodermic needle was ready to plunge whenever he decided.

"I hoped you'd give up and return to the United States, or
get involved in finding that so-called missing mother of yours."

His words hit me like a slap in the face, and I felt my skin
burn with fear and anguish. My arm was numb from the pres-
ie was applying. I realized that I had to try to get control of

the situation. But how? I wasn't about to become some invincible heroine, nor did I expect the timely arrival of the police or some other savior. The only thing I could think of was to keep him talking.

"There's still time, Peter. No one ever has to know about you. You can let me turn around right now and walk down this mountain and out of your life forever. I promise no one will ever know."

God, this is so lame, I told myself. I knew he'd never fall for that. What was I going to do?

"You're absolutely right," he said. "No one will know. And that's because you'll probably never be found. You'll just be another missing American. You have no family; no one who cares where you go. Oh yes, there's that annoying, nosy aunt of yours. But what's she going to do? Go complaining to the guards?"

He chuckled at these insights. In the moonlight, his eyes looked like pools of pure blackness. No light shone there.

"And if you are found," he went on, "you'll be full of morphine. Another mysterious drug-related death. That's nothing new around here. The guards will explain your death faster than they worked out Matthew's case. You don't honestly believe that they'll do anything about you, right?"

Images fired through my mind like rockets. I couldn't control them and felt my legs wobbling beneath me. This was really going to happen. *I'm about to die and there's nothing I can do about it.*

"Okay, I'm going to die. I accept that. But before you kill me, please tell me why you did it."

"Why? Because I'm the boy who received a bicycle on his seventeenth birthday instead of a car like all his other wealthy classmates. I'm the toddler whose father scolded him for wanting to play with the other kids in the neighborhood. My father was a miserly drunk. Imagine your father is a doctor and you're treated like an orphan. No hugs, no encouragement. After school, I had to clean out the kennels for the hunting dogs he kept. I took off after high school and vowed that I'd be wealthy one day and no one would have power over me like that again. It didn't take me long to learn that smuggling drugs guaranteed me a generous line of income."

Anger froze his face as he wiped the hand that clutched the hypodermic needle over his mouth.

"So, you killed Matthew because he knew that you were a drug dealer." I spoke this very slowly as I tried to put the pieces together in my mind.

"I killed Sumner because he loved that well-mannered financial advisor so much. Enough, in fact, that he was in search of her source of drugs. Sharon Dawson was a closet cocaine user, and Matthew roamed around every corner of this island day and night in search of her supplier. I have a reputation for keeping to myself, but that doesn't mean that I don't see what's going on. It was only a matter of time before he or that small time hood Allen Skye figured out my operation. I can deal with Skye in a different manner, but I had to get rid of Sumner."

"How did you do it? Matthew probably knew this island better than you do."

"He was so blinded by his love for his Sharon that his head was in the clouds half the time. All I really had to do was walk right up to him in an unguarded moment. We struggled, and he fell and smacked his head on a stone." His hand tightened on my arm as he continued. "The hit on the head stunned him for a few minutes, so I was able to inject the cocaine behind his ear and stuff the vial into his pocket. After that it was easy. Long story short, he went over the side of the cliff. Too bad he didn't heed the warning signs. Something he should've taken into consideration before his moonlit stroll."

And Sharon Dawson? You killed her as well, didn't you?"

"I had to. Her habit had gotten worse. After I killed Sumner, she began to unravel quickly. So, she was a risk. Of course, I had to get creative. Wrapped the nylon around her neck. Made it look like suicide."

His matter-of-fact tone of voice sent chills down my spine. There was no remorse, no fear, no empathy.

"But how did you meet her? Was it through the newsletter?"

Peter laughed.

"I met her on the island one day when she visited Sumner. She'd seen him talking to that teenager Lucia, and in a jealous rage Sharon threw herself at me. It was easy to fuel her jealousy and need for attention. I immediately saw her value as a conduit for laundering money, drugs, and sex. Hooking her was simple. As time went on, my payment demands became greater."

He paused to laugh again.

"And her talent as an investment broker was immeasurable. My portfolio has swelled under the information she provided. In the end, she was enthralled to me like a wanton female vampire to Dracula. Just like you Star. I fooled you. It would only have been a matter of time before you became one of my obedient subjects."

"My accident in Dublin and the note? That was all you wasn't it?"

"You've been trouble right from the beginning. I'll enjoy getting rid of you. Miss Star O'Brien, all independence and know-how. I enjoyed playing the sympathetic ear just to watch how your stubbornness gets in your way. Yeah, it was me. And you laid it all out. I just had to show up."

"And on the Sumner's boat the other day. I was sure I detected footsteps."

"That was me too. I considered making it look like an accident where you got rammed on the head with one of the masts and fell overboard. But that might have been too suspicious, so

I decided to wait until I had you here on my territory. You have to admit that I outsmarted you."

His narcissism seemed boundless—so I decided to play to it.

"Yes, you really had me fooled. I was impressed by your concern and generosity for others. But why Peter? Okay, so you had a few rough bumps in your childhood. But you're a successful business man now."

"And I intend to stay that way. Don't think I'm going to fall for the flattery. It won't work. But I've enjoyed making a fool of you."

He raised the needle as he grinned sadistically. In a rush of frantic thoughts, I wondered why hadn't I seen this coming. Why hadn't I seen beyond the jewelry, the car, and the smoothness? The signals had all been there, but I'd missed them. Always calling after something happened with him—volunteering to drive me to Dublin, acting like he supported my independence, delving into what had happened to Matthew, asking me questions about my family and when I'd be returning to the States....

There was nothing else for me to do, so I opened my mouth and began screaming as loudly as I could. Each one came from deep within my soul, pouring out of me like a foghorn in the mist.

Then there were other screeches. Peter loosened his grasp on my arm as he cast a glance around for their source. I chose that moment to throw myself at him, aiming for his midsection and attempting to knock him down so I could run for help. But my sneakers slipped on the wet grass and my arms pinwheeled in the air as I tried to keep from falling. Too late—my weight along with the inscrutable nature of gravity directed me straight toward him.

Perhaps it was the angle at which I hit him. Perhaps he was vn off by the cacophony of screams echoing through the air. Or perhaps he just lost his footing, as did I on the wet grass only seconds before. Whatever the reason, I watched in astonishment as he became the latest victim of the cliff erosion that the signs warned of.

He fell back in slow motion, his arms flailing as he tried to grab something and found only thin air. Then he disappeared over the side of the mountain and plummeted to his death.

CHAPTER 29

A heavy silence hung in the air of Davitt's restaurant—
similar to the dense fog that drifted through the streets
outside—as Lorcan, Aunt Georgina, and I sat in one of the
booths.

"Have the guards finished with all their interviews and
statements?" Lorcan asked as he methodically worked his way
through a mound of mashed potatoes and boiled ham. Aunt
Georgina had invited him to join us. And for once, I didn't have
the energy to protest his presence. It was kind of comforting to
watch him enjoy his food.

"They're finished with me," I said, picking at the brown
bread and vegetable soup that Aunt Georgina had ordered for
me. "I met with Bridget this morning. Ironically, the initial toxi-
cology report was correct—although not because Matthew was
a slip in procedure and Matthew's results got mixed up with
some drug user. Her brother's reputation is cleared. But we all
know the damage created by the original newspaper accounts
and speculation can never be fully undone. Some people will
always wonder."

"The newspapers don't matter," Aunt Georgina chimed in
sat back and smiled. "Think about how relieved his

family is to know the truth. Your intuition about his innocence was right all along—thank goodness you decided to get involved."

I nodded. "I know. Bridget is already working with a gallery in Dublin to show Matthew's work. And I was right about the last painting he was working on. The clouds and sky were a map of Clare Island and its coves. He used a technique called displacement painting to create a path to the lighthouse keeper's cottage. That's why there was such a contrast between the sky and the clouds and the colors in the painting's foreground." I shook my head. "I only wish I had figured everything out the first time I saw it."

"What about Peter?" Lorcan asked. "Did he have any family?"

"None, that the police can find," I replied. "He told me that his father was a doctor. It sounded like he was also a strict disciplinarian and not too nurturing. But it appears to be a dead end. They've been able to trace him back to the time that he served in the Navy. There's some speculation that while he was in the service, he was approached about transporting drugs, and that may be when he began his career as a smuggler. Which reminds me," I looked at Lorcan directly, "when Peter and I met you at the Kirk Restaurant, I saw the way you stared at him. Did you two know each other?"

"Still doubting me Star?" Lorcan asked. "No, I didn't know him, and you're right about the look I gave him. But don't you think I'd want to check him out? Here he was out with Star O'Brien, the one person I know who is so independent that she's very picky about her friends. That's all it was."

"His lifestyle provided the perfect cover for his activities," Georgina said. "Who would ever have suspected him? He was so charming and concerned about people." Her warm brown eyes held me in her gaze, but I could only frown back.

"Let's not discuss his charms, Aunt Georgina. I never

suspected him. Of course, he never mentioned knowing Matthew or Sharon. In fact, when I first met him on the island, he acted like Matthew was a stranger. Who would have entertained the idea that a successful entrepreneur and community benefactor needed or wanted to be involved with drugs? I only wish I'd been more perceptive." I shifted in my seat, feeling trapped by the furniture around me, and glanced over at Lorcan before looking down at my now-cold bowl of soup.

"So how did Hughes go from the Navy to owning an expensive piece of property and lighthouse on Clare Island?" he wondered. It was nice to see that he didn't seem interested in rubbing my nose in my mistakes for once.

"After the Navy," I began, "he put himself through business college and earned a real-estate agent's license. Former co-workers said that they suspected his activities in the homes he listed for people." Lorcan seemed confused by this, so I quickly added, "It turns out he used the empty houses as pick-up points for the drugs. Later, he got involved in shipping pieces of antique furniture from Europe, and the police say he may have been smuggling drugs in those as well. The lighthouse, the newsletter, and the antiques business provided an ideal front for running a multimillion-dollar drug operation."

"And sure enough Clare Island offered a perfect place for boats and shipments around its coves," Aunt Georgina said as she waved to the waitress to bring more tea.

"I suppose Matthew got involved while he worked on the island restoring the Abbey," Lorcan suggested.

"Not exactly," I shivered, my mind replaying images of Peter and our conversation. "Peter met Sharon one day on the island. She and Matthew had just had an argument about the time he'd been spending with Lucia. And Peter seized upon Sharon's vulnerabilities regarding her relationship with Matthew to further his illegal activities. As time went on, her habit got e and she began exchanging sex for more drugs."

I pushed the soup around the bowl with my spoon before continuing.

"Matthew knew that Sharon had a dependency problem. The police found a letter from Sharon to Matthew threatening to break off their engagement if he chose to intervene. The police surmise that when he couldn't persuade her to get help, he focused on finding her supplier. That led him to Allen Skye, which in turn led to the knowledge that there was a bigger operation in the area. Matthew may have even caught Peter in the act. That part isn't clear. Peter indicated to me that he'd taken the initiative before Matthew put all the pieces together. It's possible that was Peter's egotistical personality speaking. Who knows what the truth really is? The bottom line is that he killed Matthew first, then decided Sharon was too big of a risk and killed her, too."

Lorcan paused long enough from his attack on his food to say, "I suppose he was behind the anonymous note and the car that attempted to run you down in Dublin." Then he smiled at me before he turned back to his potatoes. Why hadn't I noticed the warmth of his smile before? I wondered as I sank further down into the cushion.

"Yes, he wanted to have an inside track into the investigation, and he focused his attention on me. I don't know what else to say. I was beguiled by his charm."

I plunked my spoon down onto the table. Who was I kidding; I had no appetite.

Aunt Georgina sternly took stock of me over the top of her teacup. "Listen to me, Star O'Brien. I won't tolerate any self-pity. You pick yourself right up and move on,"

I nodded in semi-agreement. "Finding my birth mother seems to be a dead end as well, Phillie had a lead about a woman in Cong. But when I phoned, I found out she's away on holiday for an extended period." I hesitated, then decided to plow ahead. "You're right about one thing, Aunt Georgina. It's time to move on. I'm closing up the cottage and returning to the States next week."

The tea sloshed over the rim of her cup as she slammed it back into its saucer.

"What! Jeepers, Star, you can't leave! That's not what I meant!" Then she turned to Lorcan. "Isn't it time you told her? Stop eating, for God's sake!"

Lorcan placed his fork on his plate and leaned back in his chair. His eyes surveyed both of us.

"Star, I know how much you resent my involvement in your affairs."

"Absolutely," I replied as I sat up straight and prepared to bolt.

"Well, hear me out...." He pulled an official-looking letter out of his shirt pocket. Then, pushing his glasses up on his nose, he said, "The Director of the House of Birth Records is a personal acquaintance of mine. He's offered to help you with your search for information on your mother. Now, it doesn't mean that you'll find anything. There's a good chance there isn't a record in Dublin. But, Star, I know you won't quit until you've investigated this as far as it leads you."

He grinned at me from across the table as he refolded the paper and placed it in his shirt pocket.

"I don't run away from anything, Lorcan McHale," I told him firmly. "How dare you imply that I'm a quitter! You know what? The States will still be there, but I'm not leaving Ireland until I have some answers!"

The grin spread across his face while Aunt Georgina called for another pot of tea.

Damn him. He knew I'd rise to the bait.

ABOUT THE AUTHOR

MARTHA M. GEANEY is the author of the highly praised non-fiction, women's leadership book, *Bring Your Spirit to Work: One Woman at a Time.* She is also the author of the Star O'Brien fiction series  which is set in the west of Ireland, and the United States. Martha was born in New York City but lived in New Jersey beginning at the age of eight. In 2017, Martha and her partner, Bill, moved to Florida where she enjoys cooking, reading, swimming, and her Schipperke puppy, Turlough.

Before turning to indie writing, Martha was a teacher, management consultant, university professor, and the dean of a business college. It was her leadership experience as a management consultant and her research for her doctorate that prompted Martha to write a self-help book for women who aspire to leadership roles.

Martha's passion for Ireland began when she made her first trip, at the age of four, to County Mayo, birthplace of her mother, and to County Cork, birthplace of her father. She returned to Ireland again at the age of sixteen to attend a boarding school in Castlebar, County Mayo, for two years. Since then, Martha has visited her cousins and friends in Ireland for more than thirty-five years. It is her love for the people, the country, and all its beauty that inspired her to create a mystery and suspense series, set in Ireland, about an amateur detective, Star O'Brien, who is an American.

She is currently working on her second Star O'Brien novel.

AND A FINAL NOTE FROM MARTHA—

Thank you for reading *Death on Clare Island*. I hope you enjoyed meeting Star. If you have time, please leave a review on Amazon.

And if you have questions or feedback that you'd like to share, please contact me at www.martha-geaney.com. I'd love to respond to your comments. You can also post feedback at facebook.com/marthageaneyauthor.

Lightning Source UK Ltd.
Milton Keynes UK
UKHW020603070819
347545UK00006B/118/P